LISTENING TO

To Mary

Love, Sue Pacey x

Sue Pacey

Michael Terence
Publishing

This edition first published in paperback by
Michael Terence Publishing in 2020
www.mtp.agency

ISBN 9781913653200

The dedication for this book comes from those who inspired it – my wonderful NHS family. Some have moved away and gone on to other things. Some are very much still in both my life and my heart. The love we showed each other has grown and flourished to this day.

Chapter One

"Hello, my favourite little sweetie, and how are you today?" the kindly old man said leaning back in his comfortable leather chair. I smiled gleefully, my eyes wandering to the jar where he kept the sweets. He winked and reached for the jar, shaking a few jelly babies out on the desk and pushing them in my direction. I munched for a few seconds. He regarded me over the top of his half-spectacles as he always did.

"Now then, what's this your mum tells me about these special friends of yours?" I was comfortable with him – our doctor. He'd been there on the day I was born, thrust howling into this world and it seemed he'd been a part of our family ever since.

He was a big man even compared with other adults, but to a little girl like me he seemed huge. A mop of grey hair sprouted in all directions from his scalp, joining at the sides of his head to become a greying, and equally unruly beard, that came to rest on his chest. Underneath lurked a red and white spotted bow tie, but you only got a glimpse of it now and then when he turned his head. When I was older, I used to count the times I caught sight of it at any one sitting. He only had one eye and wore a black leather patch. I remember wondering if he was really a pirate. His tweed suit had seen better days, the elbows sporting leather patches that matched the eye patch. He had a very large stomach on which his hands rested, fingers linked, when he spoke. A daunting sight, but I was completely unafraid of him.

Thoughtfully I bit the head off a green jelly baby.

"Mum tells me you have a special friend, but only you can see her. Is that right?" He spoke in that matter-of-fact way doctors use when trying to get information without you realising you're telling them anything.

"Yes," I replied, busy with another sweet. "Her name is Lily."

"Do you think I would be able to see her?" He took off his half-glasses and carefully placed them on the blotter in front of him.

"Course." I pointed to the small chair beside him. "She's sitting there."

His eyes moved sideways to the child-sized, rattan chair. I looked at my Mother. She was looking at it too.

"What is Lily doing at the moment?" he asked casually.

"She's laughing," I said.

"Why do you think she's laughing?"

I giggled. "Because you can't see her."

He paused and rubbed his beard thoughtfully. "Would she like a jelly baby?"

I looked at Lily and she nodded furiously in anticipation.

"She's not allowed them," I told him, "Her Mother says they'll make her teeth bad!"

Lily frowned, her little mouth set in a petulant pout of indignation.

Dr Richie leaned back slowly in the chair and looked from my Mother to me, then to where Lily sat swinging her legs to and fro.

"I wouldn't worry too much," he said to my Mother with a wry smile. "I think she'll grow out of it. A lot of kids have imaginary friends. What is she? Five? I bet by the time she's six it'll been replaced by something more exciting. After all she had a rocky entry into this world as I remember. With that umbilical cord wrapped around her neck four times, she must have got a bit short of oxygen." He huffed and shook his head. "I know I did, pulling her out." He laughed. "Maybe the experience heightened her awareness instead of damaging her. She's just a bit different that's all – and with a fertile imagination to boot. Probably grow up to be a doctor or perhaps a novelist!" They both laughed heartily and we left.

According to my Mother, it seemed that, from a very early age, I certainly was different.

Looking back, I suppose everyone feels a bit unusual at some stage. It's called growing up. As kids, we generally get over it quickly and move on to teenage spots and even spottier teenage boys. That's unless something happens that is so life-changing it affects us more profoundly. Nevertheless, a child psychologist would probably have had a field day. And, as a well-known character in a successful TV series once said, 'I couldn't possibly comment!'

I certainly wasn't aware I was any different from anyone else – not then anyway. I assumed everyone was like me and saw and heard the same things I did. Even when I did start to realise, I thought it was others who were out of step, not me. Far from being threatening and uncomfortable, I was very happy with it. It has always made me feel special and I fervently hope it never goes away. This ability has made me the person I am. Without it, I just wouldn't be me any more.

The thing is, I see and I hear people others can't – dead people! Always have for as long as I can remember.

When I was twenty – it took me that long to pluck up the courage – I actually asked the opinion of a psychologist. He was a colleague so I didn't have to make an appointment, which was fortunate, or confess it was me. He assumed it was purely professional interest about someone else. He said most children, at one time or another, have imaginary friends who they talk to, play with and pamper in a manner usually reserved for the family dog. These little 'playmates' can be useful to the child, often getting the blame for little indiscretions. Parents, on the whole, are largely tolerant and humour their offspring by setting an extra place at the table and patiently including 'Henry' or 'Abigail' in plans and even conversations. 'Fathers', my colleague told me, 'often get fed up with the charade first!' It was his view that children with a tendency to behave in this way are often 'singletons, bored, lonely, rather unloved and unhappy'.

That was somewhat confusing. There I was breaking the accepted rule again! I didn't fit any of his criteria.

***

I had a wonderfully happy and loving childhood though money wasn't in great supply. Dad was a machinist at the local steelworks and Mother was a stay-at-home mum. All the privileges in my upbringing came from a family where love was given freely and without question to anyone who stepped over the threshold.

What did it matter if by the end of the week there wasn't a shilling left for the gas meter? Was it important that your clothes came second or third hand? It was having some, not where they came from!

There were two sets of kids in our house, mum and dad having started again with the breeding programme in their forties. My older sisters were thirteen and fifteen years older than me, respectively.

Every morning before going to work, they fought like a couple of cats!

In fact, one of my earliest memories was my Mother throwing them both out into the garden still scrapping furiously, closely followed by her slippers in case they upset 'this 'ere bloody baby!' It was years later I realised the 'bloody baby' was me – and she was a very good aim with those slippers!

My younger sister, Janet, Nipper as she was known, put in an appearance when I was six and we were to fight with the same ferocity as our older sisters before us. It never ceases to amaze me how our parents stayed sane. Our little 'two-up-two down' cottage must have been bursting at the seams until the older two left home.

Then, there was our psychopathic mongrel, 'Blackie', who was actually brown. Maybe that was his problem, he had an identity crisis!

We shared a back yard with the adjoining cottages, bounded by a six-foot wooden fence with a gate to prevent us all escaping. However, no-one stood a chance of getting out as the dog saw to that. He was more than happy to allow anyone in, but he took a very dim view of their leaving. He would snarl with bared teeth, rooting them to the spot in blind terror. It wasn't just strangers either, the family had to have a plan of action too.

Someone had to stand by the gate and yell 'Cats!' The dog would then go completely berserk and shoot up the garden in pursuit of some non-existent moggie.

Seizing the opportunity, my Mother would grab us children and escape out of the gate, often a mere two seconds before the dog, realising he'd been duped again, hurled himself at the gate. It was often a very close-run thing!

We lived in a tiny village with three pubs and a Post-Office which doubled as the village store. There was a phone box outside the park and a rickety old bus that ran to the nearest town every couple of hours. If fortune was smiling on you, it brought you back again. No-one really had home telephones then, so that was it when it came to communication with the outside world.

Our little village was an idyll, surrounded by streams, woodland and fields as far as the eye could see. I thought it the most beautiful place on earth. The countryside was my playground, safe and familiar, with all my friends. The most special of all was Lily.

She was Irish and had that lovely lilting voice you felt could easily be set to music. Her vibrant, red curly hair cascaded down her back. How I wished I'd been allowed to grow mine long. We spent most of our waking hours together and often she'd stay over, sleeping in my little bed where we would talk until the wee, small hours, until exhausted, we fell asleep.

The six-year gap between the 'Nipper' and myself seemed half a lifetime. We had little in common. Lily and I got on far better.

One day we were playing in the garden, shrieking with laughter. Lily was pushing me on the swing, higher and higher when the woman from next door popped her head over the fence, not for the first time that day. She stood watching us curiously for what seemed like ages as we took turns at pushing and forgot she was there. Every now and again she kept asking me who I was talking to.

"Lily of course!" I said and after a while, she stopped watching us.

There followed a long series of whispered conversations over pots of tea in the corner of our kitchen between my Mother and the lady-next-door. They abruptly stopped whenever Lily and I went in for a drink or to use the toilet. My Mother gently explained that the 'missus-next-door' couldn't see Lily and perhaps it would be better if I didn't talk to her when she was around. I remember thinking what a silly woman she was and why didn't she get some glasses?

Soon, Lily came to play less and less but when she did, we were always careful not to play near that 'short-sighted missus-next-door!'

However, from that moment, I decided not to discuss any more of my 'friends' with the grown-ups.

***

As I grew into early adolescence, any mention tended to provoke an angry reaction, even from my extremely tolerant and mild-mannered Mother. It was beginning to dawn on me that no-one else could see these special friends of mine. I didn't want to be thought of as a strange child, even at that age. I just wanted to be the same as anyone else. But, I knew I wasn't and quickly learned it was better to pretend they didn't exist – as far as the rest of the world was concerned anyway.

Older and wiser people tell you, it's all your imagination and you'll 'grow out of it'. Anything lacking an immediate and plausible explanation is viewed with cynicism and your will to survive ridicule makes you suppress and deny it.

All ability, whether physical, musical of psychical requires practice to develop and improve. In short, if someone takes away your violin, you have little chance of becoming the next Nigel Kennedy!

One day, fate intervened in the shape of two broken bottles of milk!

***

Wednesday was rice pudding day! Mother used to cook it for hours in the side fire oven. I can still smell it now and my sister and I used to fight over who got the skin and all the hard, crispy bits around the side of the dish.

"It's my turn for the dish today!" I told Nipper firmly whilst mum fetched the milk from the cellar. We didn't have refrigerators until years later. It was an opportunity to state my case whilst she was gone. I was thirteen now and, in my opinion, grown-up enough to hold sway when no-one else was listening. In response, however, the little beast opened her mouth wide and threw back her head in an almighty howl.

"Waaaaaaaaaah, mum, she's hitting me again!"

This brought my Mother running up the cellar steps to the aid of her latest-born child, a bottle of milk in each hand, but in doing so tripped over the cat, who was lurking around, interested in any milk which happened to be going spare. Both bottles became airborne, covering the entire kitchen in milk, much to the delight of the cat! Enraged, my Mother picked herself up, which is no mean feat when surrounded by broken glass, milk and cat and with a shriek, proceeded to beat me around the upper body with her slippers.

Milk from the now sodden slippers sprayed in every direction with each swing. That little beast knew exactly how to get her own way!

"Just you wait till yer Father gets 'ome, then we'll see who's a bully then Madam!" Her face was puce, black gimlet eyes flashing as she moved quickly to where I had taken refuge behind the armchair.

"And you can get yer coat on and go and get some more milk and be quick about it!" she shrilled at me, still waving the slippers.

Sobbing, interlaced with short intakes of breath issued from the now pouting, though triumphant form of my small sister. My Mother's gaze softened instantly, as she scooped her up, clutching her against her breast. Over mum's shoulder, the little beast gave me a smile. It told me in no uncertain terms, that today she was not only guaranteed the skin off the rice pudding, but all those crispy bits as well.

It was half-day closing and I had to walk to the Co-op Milk Depot, a good forty minutes away, as she wouldn't give me any bus fare as a punishment. It was a bit harsh, I thought, considering I was only asking for what, on this occasion, was rightfully mine.

I had never actually been to the Milk Depot before, well not on foot, but off I went anyway still feeling aggrieved and imagining ways to get my own back on the little witch, who had deprived me of my Mother's undivided attention, by being born. That thought occupied the entire outward journey and I bought the milk and set off for home.

To this day, I don't know why I went down a different street to the one I came up. Perhaps I was meant to. Quite suddenly I found myself standing outside a small green door, with rather old and peeling paint. I just knew that if I never did anything else in my life, I must go inside.

Rice pudding quite forgotten, I pushed open the door to reveal a dimly lit winding staircase beyond. With my heart beating like a galloping horse, I took a deep breath and went up into the gloom.

At that instant, fear dissipated to be replaced by incredible anticipation. It's the feeling you get on a roller coaster when you are on the crest of the big drop; you know what's coming but it has an inevitability about it!

With a shaking hand, I opened the door at the top of the stairs and found myself in a Spiritualist Church at the start of a service. I quickly sat down at the back before anyone saw me and asked what I was doing.

My Mother had once taken me with her to have her tealeaves read and the whole episode has been cloaked in secrecy.

"For God's sake don't tell yer Father," she had warned me. "He wouldn't understand at all." I couldn't understand what all the secrecy was about, but got the impression Dad would view it on the same level as communing with the Devil.

It seemed to involve having a cup of tea, then turning the cup around three times and giving it to the old lady who we had gone to see, after handing her a two-shilling piece. I thought that it was a very expensive cup of tea: there wasn't even a biscuit.

The old dear gazed at the dregs left in my Mother's cup and closing her eyes solemnly began to tell her such amazing things as where we would go next year for our holidays and how many more children my Mother would have.

I couldn't take my eyes from the old lady's face. She was wrinkled, with a very scrawny neck and I thought she looked like next door's tortoise when it popped its head out of the shell. The old woman had a large mole on her chin, which wobbled when she spoke. It looked like a 'Rice Krispie'. I forgot everything else she had said, as I was totally focused on the mole, but I do remember that my Mother had been completely dismayed at the thought of an increase in the family. Fortunately, the old woman was wide of the mark and I was very relieved; another sister would have been too much to bear. On the way home, I was again given strict instructions not to say anything to my Father.

Over the years I had a picture in my mind of what Spiritualism was all about, as we'd discussed different religions at school. I was therefore very surprised to find no-one sitting around a table holding hands and asking if 'anyone was there?'

No-one seemed to be in a trance, or floating a couple of feet above the ground, but I had a look around, just to make sure.

I felt safe. The room was bright and airy with flowers on the windowsills and there were no crucifixes or other religious trappings like an ordinary church, save for one picture of Jesus, surrounded by little children.

The piano struck up and we sang a hymn, which I didn't know the words to, so I hummed the tune.

The lady at the front stood up and began to talk to various people in turn and they all seemed pleased and afterwards said, "Thank you." Then after looking carefully around the room, she saw me sitting there.

"Hello, my dear, can I speak to you?"

I nearly fell off my chair, but nodded. I suddenly wished I'd gone straight home as instructed, feeling that particular awkwardness that most thirteen-year-olds possess, especially when singled out for individual attention.

Much of what she said went in one ear and out the other, but I do remember her telling me that I was 'very young'. This added to my discomfort, as everyone else in the room seemed to be ancient. It didn't take a genius to work it out either; I was wearing ankle socks for Heaven's sake.

"And because you are young," she went on, "you must learn to sort out the wheat from the chaff."

I frowned. I had never really enjoyed going to the Harvest Festival and anyway we took tins of Baked Beans or cling peaches, never could I remember taking wheat or chaff, whatever that was. The lady smiled and was about to move on to someone else when, almost as an afterthought, she returned to me.

"You have a friend, with lovely auburn hair, right the way down her back," she said. "I want you to remember to always be a good friend because there will be great sadness. There is a connection here my dear," she went on gently, "talking, lots and lots of talking."

At the end of the service, I slipped out of the door quietly and down the stairs, before anyone else had a chance to say anything more to me. That had been quite enough for one day.

My wonderful and much-loved school friend Linnie, died three years later, from a sudden and devastating brain haemorrhage. It was her seventeenth birthday.

It was only as I sat looking at her in the hospital where I worked as a Cadet Nurse, did I recall the long-forgotten message from the lady in the church some three years before.

Linnie seemed to sleep so peacefully. Her long auburn hair had been brushed and thoughtfully arranged to lie across the white pillow. That lovely hair! I had never made the connection until that moment.

After all, young girls don't die do they? Not young girls like me, with all their lives before them. We had so much left to do and say and discover.

I stroked her cooling hand, gently, so not to disturb her. The lovely cared for fingernails were in stark contrast to my own, bitten ones.

As I gazed into her lovely face, with the freckles she hated so much, a small whispered voice from somewhere, said, "Good friend, talking, lots of talking."

Panic rose within me, at the remembered words, I took an involuntary deep gulp of air.

Linnie's surname was CHATTERLEY.

As I sat there, the tears came, cascading down my face, head bent forward onto the quilt, my wet cheek in contact with her still hand. I hoped I'd been a good enough friend throughout all the years we had shared.

After a while, I kissed her forehead and left her to sleep, feeling a profound sense of loss and disgust at the unfairness of it all.

Ironically, it was Linnie who first encouraged me to start writing. We had written song lyrics and one-act plays for the drama club at school. They had not been considered at all suitable, sometimes tending to be a bit racy. It was an all-girls school after all!

To compound the tragedy, Linnie's mum, heavily pregnant at the time, was delivered of a stillborn baby girl, two weeks later. Having two brothers, Linnie had been the only girl. There would never be another.

A few weeks passed and some of Linnie's close friends and myself went to see her mum, a woman pale and thin, destroyed by double tragedy. With hindsight, seeing her daughter's school friends must have been a real ordeal for her, even though she didn't show it.

As we sat sipping tea, in the front room, she said, "Lynne has taken the baby."

I desperately hoped my friend wasn't listening, but I knew very well, that she had heard and understood her Mother's pain and desperate need to find some reason for at least part of the tragedy. I said my goodbyes to her grieving family and it was done; the end of a beautiful friendship, all ties now severed by her untimely death.

It was, however not the last time I would see Linnie.

***

It was Christmas Eve. I was eighteen and the next day I was getting engaged.

Matthew and I had known each other since childhood but had not been long-term sweethearts. In fact, as kids, we had disliked each other quite a lot. One day we met again and realised that not only had we grown up, but our emotions had too. Romance blossomed.

I bathed and went to bed early, knowing that Christmas would be doubly special this year.

I awoke in a cold sweat. A glance at the bedside clock told me it was ten minutes past midnight. Somewhere far away, the midnight bells were still pealing to welcome Christmas Day. Instinctively, I reached for the glass of water I always kept by my bed and as I turned back, I saw her.

It was Linnie and she was sitting, as large as life on the foot of my bed.

With a startled cry, I threw the glass up in the air, soaking both the quilt and myself. I closed my eyes tight and shook my head fiercely to clear the sleepiness. Slowly and cautiously I opened my eyes again to see Linnie sitting there, legs crossed the way she did when we were younger. She smiled, but I could only stare, unable to believe what I was seeing. Surely I must be dreaming.

I was, however, very much awake.

"Linnie, is it really you?" I whispered fearfully.

"Of course it's me!" she exclaimed holding out her hand for me to take.

I froze, not knowing to do.

"Are you really here?" I heard my trembling voice ask.

"Of course I'm here," she replied, "You of all people must have known I would come. You have been given a special gift you know. I hope you are going to use it."

I swallowed hard, my mouth dry.

I'm sitting here talking to a dead person!

"Not really," she said, reading my mind. "I'm here and you're here and the only thing you need to believe in is your ability to use that gift. You must listen, above all listen and keep on listening."

"But what am I listening for? It was you that used to laugh when I said I saw dead people." My voice only just audible now, my mouth was so dry.

"Well," she went on, "I'm not laughing now." Linnie uncrossed her legs and sat back, leaning on her hands. "You won't always see people any more, but you will hear them."

"When will I hear them?"

"From time to time, sometimes more than others."

"Oh, God! Do I have a choice in the matter?"

"Oh, course you do, you can learn to control it," said Linnie. "You decide whether to listen or not. It's a gift, a privilege and you must never abuse it, never use it for personal gain, only to help others or it will be taken away."

"How do you know all this?"

"I know, that's all. I didn't exactly expect to be here talking to you like this."

"What was it like, Linney? What was it like to die?" She smiled ruefully.

"Strange. It happened so quickly. One minute I was there and the next I was falling down a tunnel, but the lights! The tunnel was filled with the most beautiful light you ever could imagine and then suddenly I was here with all the people I remember from long ago, folk I thought I'd never see again."

"Was there any pain? Weren't you scared?"

"Only for a moment."

"But your family Linnie! Weren't you sad? I said slowly, my eyes wide as saucers.

"Of course, but it passed. I have much more to do here than ever I did when I was there."

"Linnie, where exactly is 'here?" I ventured, half-afraid of the answer.

"Here is beautiful. It is whatever you choose to call it, Heaven, paradise nirvana; all of those things. It really doesn't matter what you call it. The only difference is that here is forever. This is where I am now, for always.

I am talking to a dead person!

The thought ricocheted around my head as I tried to take in all she said. I knew that there were things I had to ask her, for I may never get the chance again. This was impossible, I told myself. How on earth could this be happening? There was no way that this could be real, any of it.

Perhaps I am going crazy?

"No, you are not." She said in answer to my thoughts.

This time, it was I who reached out to touch her hand and it was warm. I don't know what I'd expected. She held out both her hands and I took them in mine. She wasn't cold and dead, but a living, speaking person with both substance and presence.

"Will I ever see you again, Linnie?" I whispered sadly.

"Oh, I will always be around if you need me, I mean really need me. You have so much work to do and so much to learn about yourself and what you can do with this wonderful gift. I'm only a thought away you know, but I won't come again, not like this."

"Then how will I ever know it's you?" She tossed back her long auburn hair and laughed.

"Do you remember when we spilt my Mother's perfume over ourselves, messing about in my bedroom and how we both reeked of it for weeks. Do you remember it?"

"Oh, God! Yes." I said. 'Blue Grass' wasn't it? Awful stuff."

"Don't forget it!"

Then suddenly, she was gone, leaving me alone, staring into the dark, but no longer afraid.

***

All my so-called imagined friends from childhood had been very real, but this was different. This was a friend who I had known well in life and had seen after her death. What's more, I had just had a serious conversation with her. It was a turning point in my thinking of what I believed in. Suddenly, I understood so much more. Whatever opportunities were given to me I made a vow not to waste them.

It would be a year or two before I saw Linnie again, but I always knew, without a shred of doubt that she was there somewhere, not very far away, waiting.

Chapter Two

For as long as I could remember, I had wanted to be a nurse. Actually, I had really wanted to be a dancer, but I only grew to four feet ten and then stopped, so there was no chance.

In order to get into the nursing profession in the sixties, you needed two O-Levels, to be of reasonably sound mind and have the intelligence to fill in the entry form.

When I got to the bit about religion, I chickened out and wrote 'C of E', having found from experience only too well, from overheard conversations on buses that Spiritualists were expected to levitate and go into a trance at will. Maybe we were expected to carry a ouija board to contact dead relatives whenever required to do so by the paying public.

The following thought had crossed my mind on several occasions:

Is there more money in this than nursing?

I had decided that there wasn't. Even in the twenty-first century, I still find peoples' attitude to things that they don't fully understand, extraordinary. And this, in spite of a whole television channel dedicated to the so-called 'Supernatural'.

I would gladly argue for hours on such subjects as sex and politics, but when it came to religion, I would keep well out of it. I was more than happy to leave it to the 'experts', of which there was never any shortage.

The first four weeks of our three-year training were spent in the classroom. We learned the basics of hygiene, bed making, wound dressing and anatomy, before being let loose on the wards and the general public at large.

***

Anatomy did not come easily to me.

Our tutor was a Miss Patience Appledore and her demeanour certainly did not match her name. She looked about eighty years old for a start (probably knocking on the door of sixty in reality) and wore a very old fashioned, starched cap, peaked on top, with the stiff linen sweeping downwards and across her ears like wings. She looked like a Dutch girl.

Her uniform was immaculate. She wore a silver belt buckle polished to within an inch of its life, thick lisle stockings and 'sensible' black laced shoes. The shoes, like the buckle, were shiny and the only reason you couldn't see the reflection of her knickers was that her dress came down, almost to the ground. She was as thin as a rake and had a hooked nose like a vulture. We were all terrified of her. I was sure she had been beside dear old 'Florence' herself in the Crimea.

Miss Patience Appledore, the romantic name would not have been out of place in one of Shakespeare's novels. But this was no rosy-cheeked damsel.

The word 'dedicated' had been invented for her alone. She turned bed-making into an art form. Envelope corners had to be razor sharp and measure exactly forty-five degrees, or you were 'for it'. The snowy-white bedsheet had to be turned down over the quilt by precisely eighteen inches and she did actually get out the tape measure from time to time. You practised until you could strip and re-make a bed to her satisfaction in only three minutes. It took me an age to master it. Being so 'vertically challenged' I always seemed to be paired with someone who was about five feet ten, on the other side of the bed.

Eventually, however, even anatomy seemed to have been installed in my brain, never to be released again. When one has spent so many sleepless nights learning it all 'parrot-fashion', it is in there forever.

It was so with all the other subjects we were expected to learn in that short time in the classroom. Of course, it was probably based on the fear of not passing the scrutinous questioning of Patience. She was relentless. If she passed you in the corridor, she would suddenly yell out, "Stop! Name the bones of the pelvis, nurse!" You stopped dead in your tracks and couldn't go until you had named them, word perfect, but you never forgot them after that.

We had lectures from Pharmacists, Biochemists, the entire senior Consultant staff in assorted specialities as well as the nursing tutors. The list was endless and so were the lectures for that matter.

Once, I fell asleep during a particularly boring talk, delivered softly, in monotone by a Haematologist who gloried in the name of Mr Sparrow.

My friend Shelagh, who was sitting next to me, delivered a vicious dig to my ribs when he seemed to be heading our way. I sat up with a loud grunt.

"Has he gone?"

I opened my eyes and was horrified to see him towering over me.

"No!" he thundered. "He most certainly has not gone and I will have my eye on you, young lady!"

It was delivered with enough venom that no-one dared to laugh. I stayed awake in lectures from then on.

***

Eventually 'Apples', as we called her behind her back, started to warm to us, even sometimes smiling by the end of the day. It was as though she had seen a few promising glimmers of intelligence shining through the gloom and her life's work had not been in vain after all. It was a good job too. The end of our pre-training was coming to an end and in a few days, we were to be let loose on an unsuspecting public.

When anyone sees a nurse in uniform, it is a comforting sight and people assume that you know what you're doing.

Well, it's a darn good job they didn't know the truth!

On our last day in the training school, we all huddled around the notice board on which 'Apples' had pinned the list of where we had all been assigned. Eagerly, I scanned the list for my name. I stared in disbelief. Not for me mopping fevered brows in Maternity or cuddling babies on the Paediatric wards. I was going to Psycho-geriatrics for my first experience outside the safety of the training school. I stood staring at the board filled with horror, rooted to the spot, wondering whether it would make any difference if I cried.

Everyone was talking excitedly about where they had been assigned.

"Casualty, oh, my life, Casualty, cried Shelagh hopping on the spot with delight.

"Jenny Casey and I are going to Medics." Oh, my God! Real heart attacks at last. I can't wait," Mary Neill shrieked.

"Banbury ward, general surgical. That's just what I hoped for," whispered mousy little Elaine Westry, her prayers obviously answered. "What about you Paola; where are you going?"

"Me?" I said, trying to sound matter-of-fact. "Darby Ward, actually."

Their faces became solemn, grateful I suppose that it wasn't them. Shelagh placed a comforting hand on my shoulder.

"Never mind Pao, I guess someone has to do it."

Darby ward was, in short, occupied by forty-two confused, incontinent old men, who seemed, even to my inexperienced eye, to be all on their way out of the door, feet first. I was petrified! There I was, just eighteen years old and greener than a weekend sailor in a force nine gale, realising to my horror that I hadn't seen anyone dead before. Linnie didn't count. To me, she had been asleep.

There I was about to care for forty-two poor souls who were just waiting to 'go' the very moment I set foot on the ward.

I went home and cried myself to sleep.

The next day, however, I was up at the crack of dawn, uniform pressed and starched, my hair scraped back into a tight bun, pristine apron and polished shoes. The shift started at six a.m. sharp.

I had made it and my eyes weren't too red from a night's crying after all.

I stood quivering at the ward doors, all my senses telling me to turn and run. With a sharp intake of breath, that is precisely what I did, I ran, straight into Mikey.

I really should have kept on running!

James Patrick Michael O'Halloran, (late of County Cork and of very dubious political persuasion) was my first encounter with any member of the regular ward staff. He was, as it turned out, the Ward Orderly.

He was a huge Irishman with shoulders like a weightlifter and that lovely soft lilting brogue which cannot be mistaken as coming from anywhere else. In full flow, it often sounded slightly mocking, but it wasn't. He stood six-feet-six in his socks and looked fierce enough to intimidate anyone, especially me.

Mikey looked down at my quivering six-and-a half-stone frame, his expression changing from disbelief to laughter. He threw back his head sending a mop of unruly dark curls hurtling across his face like eddies in a stream, corkscrewing this way and that.

"Jayzus! What in the name of Heaven have we here then?" he boomed, shaking the ward doors on their hinges. His gravelled voice could have cut diamonds.

"Tis one o' the little people to be sure. Well then, you just come along with me yer darlin' little child. I'll take good care of yer, so as not to let any of the big people be steppin' on yer by accident."

At this point, if the Devil himself had offered to look after me in exchange for my soul, I would gladly have signed on the dotted line.

As I was to discover later, James Patrick Michael O'Halloran would have made a very efficient second-in-command to 'Old Nick' himself.

It seemed I had arrived into the profession, even if a little unwillingly and suffering from a bad case of 'stage fright'.

I was appalled by the standard of care, in spite of everyone working like slaves and doing their best. There were only ever three of us on duty at any one time, if we were lucky and no-one went off sick. That included one qualified nurse, a student like myself and an orderly. By no means was it unusual to be left alone on the ward in the evenings, as we all had to eat. It was drudgery of Dickensian proportions, as we tried to care for all those demanding old men, keeping them dry, fed and happy, whatever that meant.

Darby ward seemed like a dumping ground for those approaching the end, folk who had nowhere else to go and few to care for them or about them.

I felt utterly useless.

Despite the floor-to-ceiling draughty casement windows that had long since been painted shut, it seemed dingy, even on a bright sunny day. The ward was long and looked as if it went on forever. There was a bathroom and sluice at either end. On each side were regimentally arranged iron bedsteads complete with horsehair mattresses, which sagged in the middle from years of use. But it was as clean as clean could be. The rows of pure white sheets (with the regulation eighteen inches of turndown) looked pristine, the green counterpanes having envelope corners 'to die for'. Old 'Apples' would have blushed with pride to know that she had taught us all so well.

So why did it smell so awful?

The smell was a heady mix of incontinent old men, poverty, unwashed clothes and sweat. The disinfectants that were used merely mingled with it and the resulting odour was one, which I still find hard to describe to this day.

As you approached to within a few feet of the ward doors, the smell hit you like a cloud which engulfed you wherever you went. It clung to your hair, skin and clothes, lodging in the back of your throat like a germ waiting to infect you. You could taste it, long after you had left for home. If you didn't wash your hair before going to bed, the smell lingered on your pillow into the next day, just in case you were to forget where you worked. The rest of the staff assured me I would soon get used to it. I never did!

Each morning the routine on the ward was the same. A sausage and bacon sandwich was given to those old men even remotely capable of feeding themselves, whilst we three frantically tried to feed porridge to the others. The more infirm old chaps, having had strokes, were often slow and difficult, unable to swallow very well. By the time we got to the third patient, all the porridge was cold. It was an impossible task which gave no satisfaction whatever and frustrated us all. Mikey summed it up perfectly.

"These old lads fought in two World Wars. A land fit for heroes! This is how we repay that courage. Confined to a bed and fed worse than animals."

The inhumanity of it made me feel sick. I was completely demoralised by the end of the first week.

It was almost impossible to keep the patients clean and dry. The 'back round' as we called it went on day and night, in an effort to keep incontinent patients from becoming sore. It was a bit like painting the Forth Bridge, finish changing the last bed and then start again at the beginning. I'm afraid there was little dignity, despite all our efforts.

I sat in the staff dining room one evening, too exhausted to eat, head slumped onto my chest, my hair practically in the coffee. I thought of the training school and dear old 'Apples' in her shiny shoes and white apron, finger-wagging to emphasise a point and I cried. Tears dripped into the coffee, diluting it. Angrily, I brushed them aside before anyone saw. I was so angry at the system.

As new students we had been taught to care, to nurse in a precise manner, slowly, dignified and with love, giving to each, on an individual basis. I thought of all those old men. Clearly, there was a huge logistical problem and no-one understood it.

How can anyone do this for long without going mad? I asked, silently to no-one in particular.

A white light flashed somewhere in my head making me wince.

Oh, not now! Go away. I thought.

"Because," said a whispered voice, just behind my ear, "someone has to do it and tonight, that someone is you, so stop blubbing and get on with it."

I looked over my shoulder and smiled, sniffing the air for any sign of 'Blue Grass," but it wasn't Linnie. It hadn't been Linnie since that Christmas Eve. How would I ever know anyway, when all I ever smelled was the dreadful odour of the ward, which I carried around with me?

Thanks, I thought to whoever it was, I suppose I needed that!

Mikey, it seemed, had decided to take me 'under his wing', like a fussy Mother hen with her newest chick and we had been paired together for the 'back round'. I was grateful for his muscles when lifting partially paralysed patients. Confused old men were not always compliant and tended to struggle.

It was an unequal arrangement, as being much smaller than Mikey, I had to clamber on to the bed to match his height and equalise the lift. The more frisky old chaps thought this was wonderful and I quickly became adept at hopping off again just as speedily, to avoid being molested by elderly roving fingers.

Mikey had a set of rules, which he felt were his duty to pass on to all new nurses. He could be seen consulting his notebook from time to time and you knew a new intonation was coming your way.

One such rule was delivered to me solemnly in the sluice whilst we were cleaning the bedpans. "Never accept gifts from strangers, or in this case, patients," he said, wagging his finger as if to a naughty child. "After all, is that not what yer Mammy used to tell yer? Well little one, pay attention now, because I'm tellin' yer the same."

I nodded, so why didn't I listen?

Late one evening, a lovely old gentleman beckoned me over. Though he only had the use of one side of his body, he had never lost his twinkling smile. He had the bluest eyes I had ever seen.

"What is it, love?" I asked.

"Sweeties for my favourite nurse," he said, reaching into the bedside locker with his good hand.

"No Mr Marshall, I couldn't," I said, "You save them for yourself," but he was already pressing the thick paper bag into my hand, his fingers closing over mine.

"Can't eat 'em lass! Anyhow the buggers have taken me teeth away!" he exclaimed with a gummy grin. So, giving him a quick peck on the top of his bald head, I stuffed the bag into my uniform pocket and hurried off to catch the bus home.

Sitting on the top deck in the warmth, I began to doze. All at once, I remembered the sweets. As soon as I pulled out the now slightly soggy bag from my pocket, I knew something was wrong. Gingerly, I peered inside.

It was poo! Human faeces rolled carefully into little balls the size of Maltesers. I was horror-struck and for a moment didn't know what to do.

The 'gift' for his favourite (and very stupid) nurse, had now come into contact with the air. The other passengers were rapidly becoming aware that a disgusting and instantly recognisable smell was coming from my direction.

I looked around furtively and tried to pretend it wasn't me. A few of my fellow passengers had the decency to examine the soles of their shoes. Most of them simply glared at me, before moving as far away as is possible on a crowded bus at chucking out time. Mortified I sank down in my seat and stared miserably out of the window, carefully pushed the bag back into my pocket, swallowed hard and tried not to think about it. At the next stop, I leapt from the bus, not daring to look right or left and walked the rest of the way home in the pouring rain.

I made myself a solemn promise to listen to Mikey the next time he gave me advice.

***

I had overslept. I was late for work. The usually reliable bus hadn't come.

Probably had to fumigate it! I thought.

My hastily tied up hair was refusing to defy gravity and my cap wouldn't stay on. We wore little white detachable collars, which buttoned on to the dress. They were stiff with starch and took the skin off your neck within a couple of days. This was the day that the button was destined to fly off.

I eventually arrived on the ward late, hot, panic-stricken and looking like the victim of a nasty mugging. I was convinced that Sister, whom I had not yet met, was going to kill me and my short career as a nurse would be over before it had begun.

"O Jayzus! You are in fer it child," droned Mikey solemnly as I flew past him. "Let me tell yer that 'Herself' is in a particularly vicious mood this day, so she is."

I closed my eyes and swallowed hard, feeling hotter than ever. Sister was, after all, one step away from the Almighty, dangling your fate as a nurse in her hand. You did as you were told, straight away and without question.

It was only a few years ago that junior nurses had to bob a curtsey as she went by. The ward was her domain and the fate of the patients rested in her hands. She was responsible for everything, from the visitors to what went into the pig bins, which, incidentally, she inspected daily. You could have been forgiven for thinking that the Doctors were in charge, but even the Consultant knew his place. He was fully aware that he was a guest on her ward and was there under sufferance. The junior medical staff were terrified of her.

As a junior nurse, you did not speak to Sister unless spoken to and the only time you found yourself in her office was when you were summoned or when you were late.

I hovered outside the office door, trying to pluck up the courage to knock and wondering whether to practice my curtsey.

"Well girl," boomed a rather deep female voice, "Come in. Don't be standing out there shaking all day long now!"

Sister Hedera Monaghan was the kindest, sweetest soul I had ever met. Far from the blasting I'd expected, I got tea and toast spread with her home-made plum jam, which she kept locked up in the bottom drawer of her desk. Only later did I learn that it was hidden to prevent a certain Ward Orderly from getting his thieving 'paws' on it.

Sister Monaghan was a large woman with broad shoulders, but with not an ounce of fat on her frame. At six feet tall she cut an imposing figure. Her dark blue uniform, with its long sleeves and white cuffs, had not a single crease, even when she sat. Her waist was tiny for one so tall, her belt clasped with an ornate silver buckle, decorated with snakes twining around a branch. I couldn't take my eyes off the beautiful thing. Her ruddy complexion suggested the outdoor life of a farmer's wife, the face fringed by greying hair, pulled back and fastened in a severe bun.

Her head was crowned with a fine, linen cap, which fell in intricate pleats down her back. It must have taken hours to fold.

When she spoke, it was with the same Irish lilt that I had heard somewhere before and there was a mischievous twinkle in her eyes whenever she smiled. However, her reputation went before her and I never doubted that she was more than capable of turning into an absolute tyrant if the situation called for it. She could wither strong men at a glance, ruling both her ward and the doctors with a will more effective, than a loaded machine gun. Fortunately, never was it pointed in my direction. She would yell, "Nurse!" at the top of her voice and you came, even though the words were softened by the Irish lilt. There was something very familiar about her, for she was, by sheer accident of birth (God bless her) the older sibling of none other than James Patrick Michael O'Halloran.

Mikey never failed to use this coincidence to his full advantage. No matter what he did or said, there was no way anyone was going to snitch to her and he knew it. After all, blood is thicker than water!

He liked to keep 'something on everyone', pretending to write things down in a little book. I lived for the day when fate would allow me to get my hands on his little book. I never did.

"Oh, the things I could tell Herself about yer all," he used to taunt. "Not one of yer would last two minutes here without me so yer wouldn't."

He made his sister out to be a cross between a female version of Atilla the Hun and Lizzie Bordan. None of us doubted that he wouldn't hesitate to 'shop' us if it meant ingratiating himself with her.

Hedera Monaghan adored him, knowing, I'm sure exactly what he was up to. After all, she knew everyone's next move before they themselves had thought of it. No-one got away with anything, except Mikey, who always came up smelling of roses, with his halo firmly intact.

The first week of my career came to a close. I couldn't quite believe my luck that since I came, no-one had died. I was sure it was luck and not anything to do with my nursing skills, but I was grateful anyway.

Unfortunately, this situation was not to last.

Chapter Three

The following day, I arrived at work as usual. Little did I know that this was a day I was not likely to forget easily. On this beautiful, sunny day when all was apparently well with the world, I would encounter my first 'death'.

Mikey had already put me through the initiation ceremony, as he felt was his personal duty to all new staff. This involved scaring the living daylights out of you with such tales as how the corpse has suddenly sat up during the process of being 'laid out'. His stories had been honed to perfection over the years, elaborated on and bits added to the extent that they truly belonged in the realms of folklore. This knowledge was no good to a frightened teenager such as myself when late at night, just before going home, Mikey decided to tell his gory tales. When it came to scaring anyone witless, he was a Grand Master.

So it was with some misgivings that I crept inside the ominously drawn bed curtains with my 'laying-out' trolley and stood staring at the motionless shape beneath the sheet.

"Tis okay, you will not wake him up!" exclaimed Mikey from behind me. I jumped and grimaced.

"Well now," he said clapping his hands as if starting a race, "let's be getting on with it." He slyly winked at me sensing my discomfort. "Tis only right, seeing 'twas you who finished him off, so it was!"

"He was a-a-alright yesterday," I stammered, still unable to drag my eyes from the white sheet and not at all convinced that he had quite gone.

"Ahhhh," said Pat, his eyes narrowing accusingly, "that was before you gave him those two Paracetamol that was meant fer the fella' in the next bed." I stared at him miserably, waiting for a punchline, which never came.

"Jayzus Christ woman! One week on me ward and yer've already managed to bump off one o' me patients." He shook his head sadly, setting the unruly hair in motion.

That did it. I burst into tears and fled to the bathroom almost upending Sister, on the corridor as I went. Locking the door, I sat on the edge of the bath and sobbed.

Yes, it was my fault! I had helped Sister dish out the tablets the night before and I had given the wrong ones. I had told her and she said nothing, only raised her eyes momentarily to Heaven. Oh, God! I resumed sobbing. It was my fault.

Of course, it never occurred to me that the old chap had been ninety-four, with terminal cancer and Chronic Bronchitis. That was nothing to do with it. I had killed him stone dead with my two stray Paracetamol! My misery was complete.

"James Patrick, Michael O'Halloran. Get yer worthless self into me office this instant!" came a thunderous Irish voice from outside my refuge. There followed a tremendous door slam, which should have taken it off the hinges at the very least. Drying my eyes, I crept from the bathroom. A small huddle of staff, cleaners, nurses and porters were listening outside the door to Sister's Office. The door was no barrier to the row, which made all of us jump and then Sister's voice continued in Gaelic for quite a time. There followed a huge thud, which I fervently hoped was her fist on the desk and not Mikey's nose. Then the row suddenly resumed, this time in English. "And if ever I should find yer puttin' the fear o'the Almighty Himself into me nurses again, so as He is me judge, I'll separate yer from yer breath so I will! Now, you just get yerself out o'my sight and tell that poor child the truth. If I ever were to catch yer tormenting me little girls again, you can be sure I'll be tellin' Father Rayner all about yer dark secret at me very next Confession so I will!"

There was silence and we fled.

I never found out to this day if he had a dark secret or what it was, but the threat alone seemed to do the trick. He was suitably contrite, pleaded for my forgiveness and insisted that it was just his 'little joke'. I was not easily convinced.

Half an hour later, I got over it. We had two more deaths and there was work to do.

I was duly entrusted to Nurse Mary Murphy to learn to do it properly, Mikey, being formally 'in disgrace'.

Nurse Murphy was an Enrolled Nurse and she was about fifty. The Enrolled Nurses studicd a shorter and more practical-based course for their Certificate. It allowed for girls and boys who were slightly less academic to become qualified nurses too, but they never rose any further up the hierarchy, many had been there years and were very experienced. Mary Murphy was one of these.

She was a round lady with a face to match. Any bone structure that was there was well covered by jowls of flesh, which wobbled as she went along. In fact, all of her wobbled as she went along. Like Sister, her green uniform was never less than immaculate and it was topped off with an intricately folded linen cap, the sort which we as students, were not allowed to wear. It tapered down to the nape of her neck and from under it sprang the reddest and the most unruly hair I had ever seen. It was completely out of control at all times and she spent a good portion of every day trying to persuade it back under the cap, by poking in yet another hairpin. It never ceased to amaze me, how she managed to hold her head up by the end of the day from the sheer weight. Everyone I had worked with so far, was not only twice as big as me, but they all seemed to come from the Emerald Isle.

We were just about to get on with the job which, so far I had only done in theory when, without warning, she fell dramatically (and heavily) to her knees by the bedside and started to pray. I stared open-mouthed. She opened one eye and looked at me disapprovingly, and pointing a plump finger firmly downwards, gestured for me to do the same. I obeyed, scanning my memory for the lesson on laying-out. I could remember nothing about having to pray. O I knew about treating a body with respect, handling it gently and talking to it, as if still alive. I'd learned, by heart, the practicalities of the process, washing the body and 'tying off' or 'packing' the bits which were likely to leak. But praying? Had I missed something? We had been instructed to leave the body to rest for an hour after death, in order for 'the soul to rise and leave'.

At the time I had been quite pleased to hear that, maybe they did understand after all. An hour seemed to be a decent time although I knew, of course, the soul left well before this, I had thought better of enlightening them though, as I'd have probably been certified on the spot. Frantically with my head bowed and my hands together, I tried to recall the bit about 'kneeling and praying'. Suddenly dismayed, I thought, that at the rate folk died around here, I was destined to spend the next couple of months on my knees.

A loud "Amen" brought me back quickly to the present. As rapidly as she had descended, Murphy got to her feet, crossed herself and without a word, got on with the job in hand. My initiation it seemed was over.

***

There are very few people that don't have a hang-up when it comes to death, and Spiritualists are no exception. It may be that we are able to accept it better than most.

During my four months on that first ward not only did I see many, many people die, but I learned a great deal about how others cope with the experience. Mary Murphy, a very devout

Catholic had to pray. This was her particular coping mechanism, indoctrinated throughout her upbringing and comforting her as an adult. She was despatching someone in the certain belief that her prayers would help him on his way to Heaven, and they must not go without it.

On the other hand, Mikey had to joke and quip. Although from the same religious faith, I felt that he treated it all with far more cynicism, but 'toed the line' just in case.

Quite often though, I still found his particular coping mechanism hard to take. He would stand at the bottom of a bed, whose occupant was 'on the way out'. With arms outstretched, he would whisper, "Ahhhh, the angels are hovering over this one." He would then feel at the old chap's nose and if it were cold, away he would go, like a flash of lightning to set the laying-out trolley. It was all I could do sometimes to prevent him from hanging a shroud on the bottom of the bed to save time.

Despite how this sounds, he was never irreverent, death to him being inevitable and the sooner the practicalities were done, so much the better. I swore that if he ever were to come within a yard of my nose, I'd kill him.

Working on that Ward not only taught me about dying, but it reaffirmed my faith, that death is not the end. In difficult moments, I have been able to draw on what I learned there sitting with the dying, holding hands and trying to give comfort. Just before death, a change took place. I witnessed it over and over again. The agitated suddenly became calm, the cares of this life were gone, pain disappeared and the person relaxed. Their attention would move away from whoever was with them to a place halfway up the wall and they would smile, as if welcoming a dear friend. Often the person would hold out their hands, their attention fixed on that, which only they could see. During this period the eyes would close gently and in a few short breaths, they would be gone.

I have seen this repeated so many times that I truly believe that someone does indeed come for you to guide you through the transition between this world and the next.

A few years ago, when my beloved Father was near the end, he was apparently unconscious, as he had been for days. My Mother, who had never left his side for ten days, was sitting by his bed, along with my sisters and myself. We were chattering, about things we had all done together as children, when dad suddenly opened his eyes. Turning his head toward us and putting his finger to his lips, he whispered, "Be quiet, he'll hear you."

"Who will hear dad," my older sister Margaret, asked gently, squeezing his hand affectionately. "Are we disturbing you?"

"Him," whispered dad, with a failing voice, "The big black fella', don't let him hear you." With the other hand, he pointed to the corner of the room. Six pairs of eyes wandered over to the spot though our heads didn't move at all.

"Go home," he said to mum, "I won't be here after today. It's time to go with him you see." With that he smiled and went to sleep, never to wake in this world again.

***

I was now one of the more experienced Students with a few short weeks under my belt. At mealtimes I was frequently left in charge of the Ward. Mikey, true to form still teased new nurses mercilessly. As with me, he was completely convincing and they believed every word he uttered, at least for a time. Either that or they were completely in awe of him, after all, he was closely related to the person who wrote their reports at the end of the allocation. Love him or loathe him though, I was very sure that all the messing around was his particular coping mechanism and he took the job no less seriously than anyone else.

When laying a body out we had been taught to make them look as nice as possible for the relatives to see, given, of course, that they were dead. We always had to remember that this was the last memory they would take away with them. If cheeks were sunken, they were 'padded out' with cotton wool, whilst trying not to make anyone look like a hamster. Vaseline was useful stuff to make eyes stay shut and a pillow strategically wedged under the chin, hidden by the covers, ensured that the mouth did not flop open displaying clouds of cotton wool.

Relatives, as a rule, did not examine too closely, only wishing to get out of the place as quickly as possible in order to grieve privately. This was providence, as Mikey had one appalling habit.

To prevent any leakage from the bladder, it was necessary to 'tie off' the penis. We used a thin piece of bandage. Mikey used to insist in tying it in a rather elaborate bow. No matter how many times it was pointed out to him that maybe some found this offensive, he insisted that the bow, with its loops, did a better job than a simple knot. The problem was that the young nurses tended to copy him, thinking this was the correct way to do it. On occasions it ended up with some poor old soul going off to meet his maker, looking as though he had been 'gift-wrapped'.

A few years later, I found myself working on an adjoining ward, helping out. I had to go over and 'check' a body. A Trained Nurse had to do this to make sure everything had been done correctly before the body was despatched to the Mortuary. There, under the shroud was Mikey's unmistakable trademark. I smiled raising my eyes to Heaven.

I saw him later at supper. Creeping up behind his back, I tapped him on the shoulder.

"Jayzus!" he exclaimed dropping his knife and fork. "What in the name of Holy Mary have we got here then? 'Tis the little person so it is." He taunted me in the usual way, as though no years had passed at all.

"Hello, you old devil, still up to your old tricks I see." I gave him a kiss on the top of his, still hopelessly unruly curly head.

"I swear by the Saints I do not know what you mean," he replied, too innocently.

I gave him my 'O yes you do' look.

Suddenly he became very serious and I had rarely seen this side of him. Leaning across the table so that no-one else could hear, he looked me straight in the eye. This was also a 'first'. He never looked anyone in the eye.

"If I should get into such a state that they ever were to incarcerate me on me own ward, will you do me a final favour?" he whispered conspiratorially.

O Lord, I thought, he's going to ask me not to let him suffer or to put a pillow over his face or something. Either that or something so dirty as not to warrant a reply.

"Go on then," I said cautiously leaning forward.

"When I go," he said, "I want to have a huge red ribbon tied up in a bloody great bow, so I can be goin' out with a flourish. Will you do that for me?"

I howled with laughter.

"The biggest and the brightest I can find," I said, meeting his gaze.

He placed his enormous hand over mine.

"Thanks, Paola, may God bless you."

It was the only time he had ever called me by my name.

In the early years of our lives, we learn by example, show how as opposed to know how. We are born into this world completely helpless and dependent on others for our most basic needs, but right from the moment of birth, are excellent copycats.

A baby of a few weeks will mimic his Mother's facial expressions. A new-born infant has full vision at a distance of 12 inches, which incidentally is the distance between his head and Mother's face when feeding at the breast. He knows his Mother and will automatically turn toward her voice and her smell, tuned in to her moods and the feel of her skin against his. When he reaches a month, his eyes are able to fully focus on her and he actively seeks her out in a room, learning her patterns of movement and how she handles him. If she is worried or anxious he will pick up on this and become fractious, his facial expressions tense and anxious. We learn to copy our parents and in this way, phobias are often passed on from parent to child.

We learn sometimes at our peril. If we touch something hot and burn ourselves we learn not to do it again, modifying behaviour as we grow, either to make it more acceptable to others or in order to keep ourselves safe.

We learn from our peers, how far to push the boundaries, what we can get away with and what we cannot.

I do not know the origins of my particular phobias, whether; inadvertently my parents passed them on to me or not.

We all have something, which we hate, something of which the very thought makes us cringe.

In my case, one of them is false teeth. They are to me, the stuff of nightmares. The prospect of actually having to handle them, still makes my flesh creep. Years later the one thing guaranteed to make me have a screaming fit, was when my daughter took out her brace and left it somewhere to be found. I am sure she used to do it on purpose. If anything were to ruin my day, it was coming across it whilst dusting, lying there like a long-dead mouse skeleton. I would not touch it, except with tongs and at arm's length.

On the ward, in the late evening, it was the responsibility of the most junior nurse to do the 'teeth round'. She had to go to each bed in turn and persuade the patients to take their teeth out for the night. They were put into individual plastic lidded pots full of Steradent and left on the locker until morning. The night staff, at the end of their shift, would put them in again, before breakfast.

My problem being that some of the old men were not able to take their own teeth out, so you had to dip into their mouths and get them. Some of the more petulant old chaps refused to open their mouths, so often you were lucky to come away with all your fingers intact. It is easy to understand why this was not the most popular job on the ward. The lengths I would go to in order to avoid this nightly ritual were, on occasions, worthy of an Oscar. There was another problem. Confused elderly men, no matter how nicely you ask them to take their dentures out, don't always put them in the pot. They were of the opinion that, because you asked for them, meant you wanted them personally and insist on dropping them into the palm of your hand. Believe me, feeling the way I do about teeth, a dose of Typhoid is preferable to the wet, slobbery, little horrors plopping into the palm of my hand.

So, it was with great relief that I found myself on duty with a very junior Malaysian nurse, one evening. At eight-thirty, drawing myself up to my full four feet ten and feeling very superior, I told her to go round the ward and collect the teeth. Congratulating myself on having avoided this awful job for another night, I treated myself to an illicit cup of tea behind the kitchen door. My joy was short-lived.

To my utter horror, I found that the girl had collected all forty-two pairs in a washing-up bowl and was nonchalantly pouring Steradent over them. Panic is a very inadequate word for my feelings at that moment. I was supposed to be in charge, not only for the welfare of the patients but also for the actions of my staff. In half an hour, coming on duty was a particularly nasty-looking Staff nurse, who already disliked me intensely, due to the fact that I had virtually upended her on that fateful day I hurried in late.

Frantically I paced up and down. The poor oriental girl could not understand the problem. My hysterical babbling, about what would happen to us if we didn't put it right and soon, were completely lost on her. I gave up trying to reason with her and grabbed the washing up bowl.

"The teeth! We must put them back in!" I shrieked at her. She looked at me as if I were mad.

What happened in the following quarter of an hour made the 'Carry On' films look like serious theatre. We raced around the ward like raving lunatics trying to match dentures with mouths and top sets with bottom sets, from the foaming mess in the bowl.

Half of the old men, confused to begin with, now believed it was morning, as we were putting their teeth in again. The other half told us to 'Bugger off!' and refused to 'open up' at all. It was sheer guesswork as to who got which and at the end, we still ended up with three odd ones left over. To this day I remain unconvinced that anyone actually got their own set and I'm ashamed to say we never owned up either.

When someone dies, one of the first things we do is to put their teeth in. This keeps the jaw shape and helps the mouth remain closed. Also, it is impossible to do once Rigor Mortis has set in.

One evening, having just despatched a lovely old gentleman over to 'Ivy Cottage', as we all called the morgue, Mikey was cleaning out the locker. I had logged the old man's belongings and was washing the bed ready for the next occupant, who was already waiting in the admission area.

With a sudden groan, Mikey clasped his hands behind his back.

"Shut yer eyes and open yer hands," he said. "I got yer a small gift, so I did."

"You must think I came down with the last shower of rain," I replied, not looking up from my cleaning. I vividly remembered the last time someone gave me a 'small gift'.

"Trust me, little one," he went on. "Tis something you'll like, I promise."

I would rather have trusted a cat with a kipper, but I humoured him. Maybe he'd found a boiled sweet or something.

Into my outstretched hand, he dropped the old man's dentures. I shuddered. We looked at each other miserably, knowing very well what it meant, Mikey the first to speak.

"Well now little one, away yer go, over to Ivy Cottage and stick them back in. I wouldn't care to be in your shoes if 'Herself' should get to find out that he went to his last resting place incomplete, so I wouldn't." I was still shuddering.

"Can't we just sort of misplace them…" my voice trailed off as I saw the look of mock offence on his face, ashamed to have thought of it.

Turning, I set off down the ward carrying them at arms' length wrapped in a tissue, my misery complete.

The very thought of having to go to the Morgue was bad enough, but replacing them in a mouth, which by now would be too stiff to prise open, I found horrifying.

Slowly, I walked out of the hospital building and crossed the courtyard, trying to stay in the lit areas and breathe slowly. It had got dark quickly tonight, or was it my imagination? All the horror films I'd ever seen came into my mind and I told myself not to be so silly. Briefly, I quickened my pace through the old oppressive Victorian brick buildings, then slowing again, not really wanting to get there.

The place used to be the old Workhouse.

What tragic and sad tales it could tell, I thought sadly. The gloom began to surround me and I ran, stopping suddenly by the door.

What am I supposed to do? Knock? Who in the name of Heaven is going to answer? Who sits in a mortuary, on the off chance that some idiot forgets to put the teeth in and comes and knocks on the door? I probably would have had a heart attack should anyone have shouted, "Come in."

There was a porter who did the mortuary duties, but surely he wasn't resident in there!

I stepped back further from the door, carefully looking around me. It was definitely darker tonight, the old building suddenly threatening and not a soul in sight.

Making a decision and taking a deep breath, I lifted my fist to knock.

The hand, which gripped my shoulder from behind, made me shriek loudly and fall to the ground, almost passing out.

I opened my eyes to see Mikey standing over me, howling with laughter, tears streaming down his face. I shrieked again, this time with relief and indignation, swiping at him as I tried to get up. In panic, I had thrown teeth and tissue over my head when he had crept up behind me.

"Go on now, little one," he guffawed, still crying with mirth. "Away back to the ward with you. Did you think I would let you do a thing like that now?"

Relief and anger all mixed into one, I ran and ran back to the safety of the ward, with its people and bright lights. Only then did I realise that dusk was just beginning to fall after all.

***

It was probably some strange form of retribution that Mikey and I found ourselves sitting side by side in the Dentist's waiting room, of all places. It was fifteen years later and I had not seen him for ages. We began to reminisce as folk do and he asked me if I recalled the incident of the false teeth. I looked around with growing mirth as it seemed the ideal place to discuss it.

"How could I ever forget?" I asked. "You scared me half to death that night. It took me years before I really forgave you." He hung his head in mock shame. "I did admire you though," I continued. "After all it was you that went in there, brave enough to complete the job."

"Brave? Nothing!" he exclaimed. "I waited a bit until you were outta' sight and I'm saying to meself, No bloody fear, James, Patrick, Michael! If he's wanting these choppers, he can come and get them fer himself. So I buried them under a rose bush and ran off home like the Devil himself was after me, so I did!"

"How could you?" I shrieked, almost on the floor with laughing by this time. After all, it was Mikey, that had nearly made me do, what he himself had been too afraid to do.

"All those years," I said, "You let me go on believing that you saved me from a fate worse than…"

"Death!" he interjected before I could finish. "Do you know that all these years I was scared shitless, in case someone should find the damn things and start digging up the rose beds looking for the rest of him!"

We fell about each other's shoulders, howling uncontrollably with laughter. Apparently, we were making so much noise, that the Dentist came out to see if the 'laughing gas' had been leaking into his waiting room.

Chapter Four

Travelling to and from the hospital, in the early morning or late at night was very wearisome. The nature of our shift pattern meant that a late shift was followed the next day, by an early one. This left little time for socialising at the end of the day. I was often so tired on getting home, that I ate, washed and fell into bed, exhausted. Studying had to be fitted in and written work had to be handed in on time. My Mother had lost count of the times she had removed books from my grasp, when late at night she had found me fast asleep, chin on chest.

A much more pressing problem was my sister, six years younger than I was, noisy and petulant and worse still, was that we shared a room. The two of us fought constantly, as our two older sisters had done in their time. My Mother was made of the stuff of diplomats, constantly walking a tightrope between us, ensuring that peace reigned for the majority of the time. It was, however becoming obvious to everyone, that long hours of studying and blaring pop music did not blend well together. This was the 'Swinging Sixties' after all.

I was not anxious to upset my Mother by suggesting that I move out. For a start, she had never let any of her precious brood leave the nest without a fight and the prospect of having to do my own washing and ironing was not attractive either. Then one day, fate intervened.

It was my day off and having nothing better to do, I'd been helping mum around the house. We had cleaned, cooked and baked all afternoon. Our Mother's legacy was that she made sure that all her girls were well-equipped for the outside world when eventually she did condescend to let us go.

We could all sew, manage what little money we had and cook from scratch. I have always been grateful for her efforts in that direction.

With pies in the oven and cakes in the tins, we were having a well-deserved cup of tea, sitting in the sun by the front window. Coming up the road from school and obviously very pleased with herself was my younger sister Annie, satchel on her back. Under her other arm, she was clutching a large violin case. I looked quickly at my Mother who was watching her progress up the path, a look of maternal pride on her face.

"Oh, mum," I said, "what has she got there? Is that what I think it is?"

"God help us, I hope not!" she exclaimed, her expression immediately changing to one of acute anxiety. "Please let it be full of books!" She instinctively reached for the teapot again, as she always did in times of crisis. My sister was now waving to us and gesturing that she had, in fact, become the proud owner of a violin.

Mother and I looked at each other and moaned aloud at the prospect of sheep's hair, scraping on cats' guts every evening for the foreseeable future. Perhaps now was the time and I took a deep breath and grasped the opportunity.

"Mum, I know you don't want to face it, but now would be a really good time for me to move into the Nurses' Home don't you think; for the sake of everyone's sanity?"

She smiled bravely and nodded with resignation, wiping her hands on her apron.

I knew I had made the right decision, when later that night we were treated to a gala performance of our family's answer to

Yehudi Menuhin. It was awful, like fingernails being scraped down a blackboard. My Mother and Father dare not look at each other during the ordeal, lest they discourage her.

Our German shepherd, Timmy, howled piteously throughout the recital, as if being tortured and thereafter, ran for cover each time she picked up the bow.

How my parents tolerated the months of practising, one can only marvel.

Annie actually became quite an accomplished violinist in her late teens, but oh, God the practising! I was eternally grateful that my own brood took up nothing more disagreeable than the triangle.

***

Three weeks later I was installed in the Nurses' Home, all my worldly goods having been transferred (and sometimes fought over,) when it came to stuff that was of doubtful ownership. Annie didn't always give things up with good grace, but the prospect of having her own room for the first time in her life obviously seemed to make some sacrifices easier to bear.

My Mother cried and I cried. My Father bit his lip and tried not to cry, whilst the dog howled. Annie, on the other hand, fetched, carried, helped with everything and generally couldn't wait to get rid of me. The speed at which she helped me unpack, at the other end, smacked of indecent haste, probably worried I might change my mind. She need not have worried; her violin playing loomed all too fresh in my mind for that.

***

The Nurses' Home was an exceptionally grim-looking Victorian building, of the kind that comprises so much of our hospital property to this day. The red brick façade was interrupted by long sash windows, popular at the time it was built, though incredibly draughty. There was no lift and as my room was on the second floor, I was to get fit very quickly.

Leaving home for the first time is overwhelmingly exciting. The freedom of being 'grown-up' cushions the blow of realising, that should you ever return home again, things will never be quite the same. The act of 'leaving' is not only physical, but a powerful emotional one too, as you take one more faltering step, up the ladder of life's experience.

My room was much smaller than the one at home, I had shared with Annie. There was a single, (and very hard) bed, made up with hospital regulation sheets and a green, sickly-looking counterpane. The bedding was made up with hospital regulation corners and a typed notice on the back of the door stated that they should stay that way. The room was furnished with a tiny bedside locker, a pull-down wooden shelf to work on, a chair and a sink in the corner. That was about it.

The carpet, a real luxury, had once been blue and had seen better days, but I didn't mind at all. This was my own little place, and I knew, that once I had added my own little bits and pieces, it would seem like home, with a lot of imagination!

In order to make the curtains stay shut you had to fasten them together with a safety pin, as they weren't quite wide enough. The hospital must have bought a job lot of fabric, as the counterpane was made of the same stuff.

The rooms on each of the three floors, all led off the main corridor, with a bathroom and toilet at either end, for all of us. You had to be a good sprinter to get there first in the mornings, if you were to get on duty by seven a.m.

It was in the 'Home', I first realised that no-one ever cleans a bath if they can help it. It took me a few days to work out that the 'plimsoll lines' round the tub, were the result of every bather having the water half an inch lower than the previous one. This presumably did away with anyone having to actually clean the thing. It seemed you could only wallow in a full tub if you were first in. If you were late, then there were two choices; roll up your sleeves and clean it, or splash around in two inches of water, like a stranded fish with the tide going out!

The often temperamental and ancient central heating system worked at 'nineteen hundreds' efficiency. On one side of the building it was so hot you could have grown pineapples and on the other side, you froze. I was billeted on the 'Arctic' side near to one of the open staircases that ran from basement to top floor. There were no such innovations as fire doors then.

In the depths of winter, when the wind whistled up that staircase, it was like being up Mount Everest in the teeth of a gale. The air rushing through the creaky old building was eerie and sounded like moaning, adding chill of a different kind to the atmosphere.

Then there were the mice. They were everywhere, despite all efforts to get rid of them. The mice were obviously of the opinion that they were there first and if anyone was going to move out, it wasn't going to be them. The quiet life that they had previously enjoyed however was about to change with the arrival of the cat.

Mitch, as he became known, was a stray tomcat, found lying in the road behind the hospital, by my friend Shelagh (pronounced Sha-lay,) who had the room next to mine. He had, apparently, been run over several times and was in a poor state. She had patiently nursed him back to health, a testament to her nursing skills. It was said by people living close by, that actually he got run over so often that he had permanent tyre-tracks on his back, hence the name 'Mitch', short for Michelin!

A very old threadbare collar and tag, only just attached to his neck, told us his name was actually 'Vesuvius', which seemed an odd name for a cat. We soon found out why.

He suffered from, what can best be described as severe flatulence and had the ability to empty a room in seconds, so not the most welcome addition to the gathering when any of us were entertaining friends.

He had only one and a half ears, presumably from fighting and teeth, which protruded over his bottom lip, giving the impression that he was permanently smiling. His fur was as black as night and he had the greenest of eyes; a real witch's cat. The second I bent to stroke him, he adopted me on sight, providing a fine sense of amusement for the few people who were aware of my particular 'talent'.

"Ah, yes, the Devil obviously knows his own," Shelagh had been heard to remark.

Pets were not allowed in the Nurses' Home and we were told in no uncertain terms that he could not stay. In order to 'champion his case', we collected all the dead mice he caught and hadn't had time to eat, in a shoe-box, strategically placed outside Home Sister's bedroom door, emphasising the extent of the problem. It did the trick and Mitch earned his keep so well in fact, that a budget was made available for his every need. This not only provided him with all the Whiskers and fresh fish he could eat, but covered his vet's bills, when he went out fighting and lost.

Home Sister was obviously terrified of mice too.

Seeing as he was now generally regarded as my 'familiar', I contributed the odd tin of flea powder and a smart new, green collar and tag. The colour matched his eyes, but I'm sure he felt a bit of a 'poser' and was only wearing it to humour me.

Mitch occasionally slept on top on the boiler in the kitchen, always with half an eye open for the odd passing mouse, but mostly, he curled up on the bottom of my bed.

When the fancy took him, he would tear up the staircase and 'meow' loudly, outside my room to be let in. If this wasn't forthcoming, he howled at full throttle, much to the annoyance of the poor girls on night duty who were trying to sleep. I'm sure he was often booted back down the stairs by the odd-slippered foot on more than one occasion.

He also scrounged from anyone who was willing to feed him and was not averse to a bit of pilfering either, if he saw anything he fancied. As the months went by, I began to get a bit worried about his waistline, trying in vain to discourage people from giving him tit-bits, but it was a complete waste of time. After all, who could resist that smile?

The cat and I spent a lot of time together when I was not on duty. It was during these shared times that I became aware of just how psychic cats are. I would lie on my bed and study and Mitch would either curl up on the foot of the bed amid piles of books, or nestle into any available space left on my lap. There was zero chance of him moving once he settled, forcing me to use him as a book rest, which he didn't seem to mind at all. Perfect symbiosis!

I would study, soothed by his contented purring, whilst he dreamed his catty dreams of mice, fish, successful conquests in territorial battles and female 'moggies'.

This situation would have been perfect, except that quite often, he would, without warning, leap into action from apparently deep sleep, hissing and growling, sending books and newly completed work flying. Leaping at the window heckles up, claws out, he would leave blood trails on my legs where he had got purchase, before taking off.

Crouched below the window, body flattened to the ground, and ears back, he prepared to face an unseen foe. Then, retreating slowly backwards after a few moments, spitting furiously, until courage restored, he made ready to pounce, hips moving side to side rhythmically. He would suddenly leap and of course collide heavily and noisily with the window.

With a howl of indignation, he would proceed to the sill, to make sure that whatever he had 'seen off' had, in fact, gone and return to his slumbers as though nothing had happened.

After witnessing this performance, at least a couple of dozen times, I began to get curious. I was also a bit worried, for if the window had been open, he would have leapt straight out and into oblivion... Obviously, he could see something I couldn't and had serious objections to its presence in his domain. The fact that he never learned from repeatedly bashing his head on the glass, showed how dimly he viewed the intrusion.

So I asked around. Did the cat behave strangely with anyone else? No, it seems he did not. Why then did he only do it with me? Everyone thought it a huge joke, except Shelagh, who had witnessed it on occasions whilst helping me study.

I had got to know Shelagh Donaghan well, as she had been an Auxillary Nurse on that first geriatric ward and had since decided to do her Nurse Training 'proper' as she called it.

Shelagh came from an extremely large family in Sligo, over on the West Coast of Ireland. She towered a foot above me and was so elegant, almost gliding as she moved along. Strawberry blonde ringlets cascaded down her back, (when they were let out from under her nurse's cap) and her skin looked like porcelain. What I would have given to have hair like that. At the time, mine was cropped short and rather boyish.

On that first ward, she would play her guitar whilst gently singing to the old men, soothing them if they became agitated. She had the voice of an angel and they loved it. Her songs worked better than any amount of medication and they fell asleep like babies. When we found ourselves in adjoining rooms, our friendship flourished.

A couple of weeks later, there was a frantic knocking on my door. I opened it to find Shelagh standing there hopping from foot to foot, face flushed with excitement.

"Whatever is the matter?" I asked ushering her in. She sat down heavily on the bed, almost upending the snoozing cat.

"Oh, you'll never believe it!" she cried excitedly. "You'll never believe what I was told, so yer won't!"

"Tell me for Heaven's sake," I said, exasperated.

"Well!" she went on, "On the ward where I'm working, we had one of the porters who was employed here years ago. Poor old soul, he's eighty, so he is and do you know, he went and tripped down the stairs and broke his two legs. He's no-one at home to look after him, so they're keeping him a while so he can get himself going again. It's a shame isn't it?"

"Shelagh, for God's sake get on with it!" I exclaimed. She often went off at a tangent like that. It was infuriating.

"Paola you will never believe what I have to tell you, so you won't."

"Tell me NOW, "I demanded, "or else I'll kill you!"

She shuffled into a more comfortable position on the bed and crossed her long legs, tossing her hair back over her shoulders.

"Well now!" she finally started the story. "I sat up most of the night with him when he couldn't sleep and he told me all about his time here and funny incidents that happened from time to time. We talked about how times had changed and from there it progressed to telling me a story about the old Matron. She was a Dutch woman, called 'Van de something-or-other, I can't rightly remember, 'twas the middle of the night." I glared at her threateningly and she continued quickly.

"Apparently, before they turned it into a Nurses' Home, this building used to be an Isolation unit for folk with tuberculosis and such-like. The old girl used to live on the premises, up here, on the second floor. She was a surly old spinster by all counts, like they had to be; very stern, a real 'old bat', who wouldn't give anyone the time of day, so she wouldn't. Her only indulgence was her cat on which she lavished constant attention and 'twas the only thing she cared for."

"Go on will you?" I said. "Apparently, 'Pussy' fell from the open window. It seems they don't always land on their feet after all. 'Twas killed of course, broke its neck clean in two so it did."

Her eyes were wide and staring, excited with the telling and clearing her throat nervously continued.

"Tis said, that the old Matron left the hospital the very next day and was never seen nor heard from, not ever again."

It was clear that Shelagh had been shaken by this strange story.

"I don't suppose I need to ask which window it fell from?" I asked tentatively, already knowing the answer.

"To tell the truth," said Shelagh slowly, becoming paler by the second, "I dared not ask. But if you were to press me…" She glanced cagily over each shoulder, "I would say that the bloody thing is still around here somewhere and it's looking for its mistress!"

I patted her shoulder and smiled.

"Leave it to me," I said, "There's nothing to fear." I knew right away why I was the only person not to have been troubled with mice in my room.

That night, I collected Mitch from the top of the kitchen boiler, took him to my room and lit a candle. Carefully placing it on the windowsill, I held him in my arms and said a prayer to anyone who happened to be close by and listening. I asked that the two of them, cat and owner would find each other, wherever they were.

Mitch roused from sleep in my arms, heckles rising briefly, then curled up in his usual spot and went to sleep, never to exhibit the strange behaviour again.

The strangest thing was, from that day, my room, which had always been chilly no matter what the weather, became much warmer.

Chapter Five

One evening, several weeks later, a few of us were having supper in the kitchen.

There had been a definite chill in the air outside, the past few nights, a herald of autumn, as if the year was slowly, reluctantly giving up the long pleasant evenings of summer.

We sat in an untidy huddle around the Aga, slippered feet stretched out to embrace its warmth.

Shelagh, ever the great storyteller, had been keeping us entertained with tales of her colourful family back in Ireland and what a fascinating lot they sounded. Most of them seemed to be of dubious character when it came to horse-trading and there was definitely a branch of the family 'from the north' who were heavily involved in 'The Troubles'. She seemed so 'matter of fact', that her immediate family were almost certainly, high up in the ranks of the IRA. Hard to believe looking into her angelic, pure complexioned face that Uncle 'so-and-so' and cousin 'whatsit' were most probably going round 'kneecapping' people, or worse, on a daily basis!

Some of her stories were probably a bit 'tall', but nevertheless, she kept us happy and laughing for hours, provided you could ignore the somewhat sinister undertones.

Mitch was agitated, prowling from lap to lap, stepping clumsily from chair to table to boiler, and back again. Finally, whilst trying to leap across the table on to my lap, he knocked Ovaltine in all directions. Everyone jumped up and scattered, to avoid the hot liquid, which dripped from the table and onto the floor, all muttering indignantly at being disturbed.

"What the hell's the matter with him tonight?" barked Jenny Jones, a somewhat bad-tempered second-year student, with long greasy hair, which matched her demeanour. "I hope the bloody thing isn't going to start farting again!" She sat down heavily in the corner of the room, crossing her long gangling legs.

Mitch's digestive problems seemed to have improved of late.

"Aw now, be nice to him," said Shelagh, furiously mopping up Ovaltine with a hankie, a smile starting to twitch at the corners of her mouth. "He's recently had a bereavement! Hasn't Pao just exorcised his only friend? Poor wee pussy!"

Everyone laughed heartily.

"Don't all start that again please," I pleaded.

I had come in for quite a lot of ribbing of late. Shelagh, sensing yet another good story to add to her repertoire, had told everyone willing to listen, about the old Matron's 'spirit cat' and its subsequent exorcism. All had found this highly amusing, only serving to reinforce the belief that I was as crazy as the cat.

Mitch finally settled himself on my knee, his stomach rolling and churning beneath my hand.

"I don't think he's very well," I said. "His stomach seems to be turning somersaults."

"I knew it!" exclaimed Jenny jumping to her feet awkwardly, legs flying everywhere, like a new-born foal trying to stand up for the first time. "It's about to fart I tell you and recycled fish is more than this body can stand. I'm off to bed." She glared at me. "I'd put it out quick if I were you."

Lifting the cat gently, I ignored her and went to bed myself, laying him on the bottom of the eiderdown. He seemed to settle but 'meowed' from time to time, waking me from shallow sleep.

"Shelagh, I'm really worried about the cat," I said at breakfast the next morning. "He seems a lot worse."

"Did he throw up?" she asked, not looking up from her porridge.

"No," I said, "But his belly's distended and he's whimpering. You don't think he has an obstruction, do you?"

"Doubt it," she said with a mouth full of porridge. "Probably ate one mouse too many!" Quickly she moved on to the toast and marmalade. Nothing ever put that woman off her food. As a general rule, most nurses are not put off by conversations of a gory nature even when dining. It goes with the job.

However, I was rather afraid that, instead of 'one mouse too many', maybe Mitch had eaten a poisoned one.

Back in my room, I crushed half a junior Aspirin and gave it to him in his milk. He lapped at it without much enthusiasm and went to sleep.

Next day, I rushed off to work, grateful that it was my half-day off, so I wouldn't be away too long. Finally, after a long morning, one o'clock came and after dashing back to my room, lifted him gently on to my lap. All afternoon his 'meows' were pitiful. He was deteriorating.

By early evening I could stand it no longer, and wrapping him in a blanket, rushed off to the Vet. Fortunately, we didn't have long to wait, as the surgery was nearly over. He was now panting heavily, each movement producing pathetic moans.

I was now convinced that poor Mitch was dying and with a heavy heart, laid him gently on the table in the examination room.

"Please don't let him die!" I begged pathetically, tears blurring my vision.

"Yours, is he?" asked the young Vet as he began to run his fingers expertly over the sick animal.

"Well," I said wiping my eyes on my navy cardigan sleeve, now generously covered in cat fur, "He sort of adopted me and we're friends. He's not going to die, is he?"

The vet smiled indulgently and gently placed his hand on my shoulder. I feared the worst and a grief-stricken howl escaped and filled the consulting room. He shook his head sadly.

With eyes closed and biting my bottom lip, I waited for the worst, fresh tears escaping from between my eyelids.

"I would imagine that you are a very good nurse," he said, looking at the uniform dress that I hadn't had time to change out of.

"Probably," I sobbed, "but it seems I can't do much for him now can I?" I must have looked a pathetic sight, mascara smeared liberally over my cheeks.

"You could probably read a cat book!" I stopped snivelling and looked at him sharply, quickly wiping my runny nose on the cardigan sleeve, leaving a silver trail.

"What?" I asked, confused.

"Let me give you a little bit of advice then," he continued, "Don't ever go into Midwifery!" I stared at him open-mouthed.

"This 'he' is a 'she' and any moment now, she's going to drop her kittens!" I continued to stare.

"But he's called Mitch!" I stated indignantly, "He's a neutered Tom."

The Vet roared with laughter, his shoulders shaking convulsively.

"Failed anatomy nurse! Look again. Now run off home and keep her warm. She's got quite a few kittens in there and the first is probably the biggest. That's what's taking her so long."

I closed my mouth finally, swallowing hard.

"Well go on," he said with urgency in his voice and handing me the cat, pushed me unceremoniously out of the door. "Now run woman. Look lively!"

I ran all the way back to the Nurses' Home in complete bewilderment, wondering how any of us so-called medical people, could have failed to notice, that our Mitch, far from being only half a fella' was in fact, a highly promiscuous good-time girl.

Panting myself now, almost as hard as the cat, I careered up the steps to the door of the Nurses' Home, only to have it held open for me.

"Thanks," I called breathlessly to the hand holding the door.

"That's okay Ma'am. After you," responded a deep American voice.

I reached the inner door, fumbling desperately to open it.

"Here Ma'am, let me get the door for you! Hey, what ya' have there?" asked 'the voice', obviously noticing the bundle in my arms. All my concentration was now on the cat, already straining with the first kitten.

"He's called Mitch," I called, over my shoulder, hardly able to breathe by now. "Open the door to the basement, could you? It's warmer down there with all the pipes."

"Lead the way," commanded 'the voice'. "Now hand him to me."

"Look," I yelled, losing patience, my attention on the cat, "Just open the bloody door, will you? He's about to have his kittens!"

Gently I placed the blanket with Mitch inside, by the pipes. I was gasping for air now, hot and perspiring.

"I'm sorry Ma'am," the voice soft and gentle now, as though explaining the simplest of facts to a small child, "but I gotta' tell ya' that if it's a boy, it ain't gonna' have no babies. Trust me. I know a little bit about these things."

"O not now!" I exclaimed, waving my arm dismissively, "I'll explain in a moment, let me get my breath back."

The first kitten was born before I had the chance, closely followed by six more, all squirming and damp, as they made their way around in search of food. We both watched in wonder and I told the story, still unable to drag my eyes from the miracle unfolding on the blanket.

When it was clear that she/he had completed the task, I sighed happily and stood up.

"Congratulations honey," said my companion, "I guess you just became a grandmomma! By the way, glad to meet ya. I'm Robbie."

My eyes followed the outstretched hand, slowly from fingertips, up the muscular arm, across impossibly broad shoulders and finally to the face of its owner. My stomach hit the floor and my knees turned to jelly. He was the most gorgeous man I had ever seen.

***

The strange story of the tomcat, which had apparently changed sex and become a Mother, circumnavigated the building like wildfire. Even the self-confessed cat-haters came by on some pretence or other, to sneak a peep at the new arrivals in the basement. No-one came empty-handed either. All came bearing gifts; an old cushion or a dish of sardines for the hungry Mother. They stood around in silent wonder in a scene akin to the Adoration of the Magi, leaving me free to recount the tale, at length to anyone willing to listen.

Next morning, exhausted by the exciting events of the previous day, I allowed myself a long 'lie-in'. There was however a downside, in that being the last to the bathroom, for once, I had to relent and clean the bath.

As I wallowed there, luxuriating, with steaming water up to my neck, I suddenly remembered the American.

What was his name? Roger? Richard? No, it was Robbie. That was it, Robbie! Where on earth had he come from? Where had he disappeared to, afterwards and much more interesting, what the devil was he doing in the Nurses' Home at that time of night? There were very strict rules; the first and last of which was NO MEN.

Closing my eyes for a few moments, I breathed the steam deeply and started to relax. Was he a figment of my imagination perhaps? I told myself not to be so silly and pulled out the plug.

Later, I paid a visit to the new family. Mitch meowed softly with obvious pride as I knelt down to stroke her gently, then purring loudly, as if to say, Look what I did, clever or what? Deceived you all nicely didn't I?

I wondered if we ought to change his name now 'he' was officially a 'she', but No! Mitch would still do very well.

She'd produced seven kittens in all; two blacks like herself, a pretty grey one sporting a white chest and paws, two tortoiseshells, a marmalade-coloured tom and a gorgeous pale mackerel tabby, bigger than all the rest. This had obviously been the first kitten; the culprit that had given her so much trouble and I knew at once that this one should be called 'Buster'.

I confess I didn't know much about cat breeding at the time, but I did know that each kitten was the result of a separate mating, so it was fairly obvious that Mitch had been out having quite a jolly time when she hadn't been catching mice.

I left them snuggling and suckling, seven pairs of tiny front paws treading their Mother's belly insistently in search of milk.

There was a note pinned to the door of my room. It said: Nurse Green, please report to Home Sister without delay.

I had never been summoned before and was a little taken aback. It usually spelt 'trouble' and turning on my heels, I ran back down the stairs without delay, wondering what I had done.

'Home Sister', as her title suggested, was responsible for all the nurses who lived in residence. She ensured that we ate properly, (to her standards) didn't stay up late, nor have too much of a good time. Her strict rules had to be adhered to, always with absolutely no compromise.

First and foremost was the rule: In by ten-thirty, sharp and one late pass a week until eleven p.m. at the weekend, but not Sundays.

Her life's work was to care for us 'like a Mother', as she saw it, in the absence of our own and let me tell you, she was stricter than any Mother. The moral welfare of her 'girls' was to be protected at all costs, hence the 'NO MEN' rule.

Just outside the main door of the Nurses' Home was an unlit alcove, which provided a really convenient spot to say 'goodnight' to boyfriends. It afforded a bit of shelter from the wind, which constantly whipped around the end of the building in both winter and summer. There was no such thing as asking anyone in for a coffee in those days! Little wonder that the Nurses' Home was known as the 'Virgins' Retreat!'

Home Sister lived with us, on the ground floor of the Nurses' Home. Her room was directly by the entrance door, so she was ideally positioned to observe comings and goings and who was doing what, at all times. If she were to hear footsteps, heading for the alcove, (no matter how we tiptoed) she would wait two minutes before leaning out of the front door and yelling at the top of her considerable voice, "Good evening, Nurse and a very 'Good night' to you young man!"

If the volume didn't send them running, the tone invariably did. She was a fearsome-looking creature who gloried in the name of Miss Florence Thistlethwaite, 'Tissie' behind her back!

If ever you were so foolish as to try and smuggle someone in, Tissie knew instinctively and was waiting; her antennae permanently tuned in to the movement of that front door. Everyone was convinced that she had some sort of bugging device, pressure-sensitive to anyone passing her door and of course, everyone had to pass her door to get upstairs.

If Tissie heard even the smallest sound of anyone creeping past after dark, out she would fly and bar the way, standing a full six feet, arms folded protectively across her ample bosom, which strained against the fabric of her long wincyette nightie. With curlers in her hair, teeth out and a liberal smearing of cream upon her face, she resembled a swamp surrounded by barbed wire. No-one would have been foolish enough to cross her.

Every night, at around eleven, she would do the 'bed round', to ensure the safety and continuing virginity of her charges. This involved her traipsing around the corridors with a flashlight, switching off unnecessary lights and calling softly, "Goodnight Nurse," at each door. She was, of course, listening intently for tell-tale sounds of illicit fun. If there were no immediate response, she would increase the call volume until you answered, by which time everyone on the entire corridor was awake.

Tissie was incapable of doing anything quietly. She was not only tall, but wide, her frame amply covered, bust and hips swinging from side to side as she 'gallumphed' along, rather like an excitable carthorse. Her raison d'être was the protection of her 'girls' and no man was ever going to interfere with any one of us, if she had her way, despite all our efforts to the contrary.

I paused briefly outside the door to straighten my hair, then knocked and was summoned in with a loud and elongated, "Cooooome."

"Hello, nurse, and how are we today?" she welcomed me with an unaccustomed beaming smile.

Perhaps this was more serious than I thought!

"Paola dear," she gushed, ushering me to a chair.

Now, this was serious! I began to wonder who had died.

"I wanted to take this opportunity to introduce you to your new neighbour."

My eyes widened in sheer astonishment. For, sitting in her best Sunday armchair, drinking coffee and eating her home-made Victoria sponge, if you please, was the American!

Tissie dragged her gaze, which seemed to border on hero-worship, away from him, to address me.

"As you can see Nurse," she went on, formality returning, "he is a man and I do not need to remind you of my policy regarding men. Men are strictly forbidden in the Nurses' Home, but this young man is an American and so the situation is different."

I couldn't for the life of me imagine why.

Didn't she remember the war for Heaven's sake when they were here in droves? What was it? Overpaid, over-sexed and over here. Did she believe that all Americans were celibate? Perhaps she wasn't around when they were handing out the nylons. Poor Tissie!

Quickly I closed my mouth, which had dropped open again, stunned into silence for the umpteenth time in two days and obviously looking nonplussed, so she went on.

"He's here on a Sabbatical to observe our practices and as we cannot accommodate him elsewhere, he will be staying in the room next to yours. I trust you will make him welcome and take good care of him my dear, whilst he is in our country."

She turned her attention to the guest, who was finding it difficult to contain his amusement.

"Robert, may I introduce you to Nurse…"

He held up his palm, cutting her off.

"Why thank you, Ma-am, but we already met. We had babies together last night!"

I choked noisily, losing any semblance of composure. He obviously did not understand that Tissie had absolutely no sense of humour when it came to any reference to sex! Spluttering I tried to recover the situation.

"C-c-cat," I stammered, aware that my face was now bright red. "The cat had kittens in the basement last night and Robbie, err– Mr –err was kind enough to help me."

Tissie's eyes narrowed. She shot me a glance like a thunderbolt and I stared at a fly making its way up the wall. Her gaze shifted once more to Robbie and she softened.

"Well, Ma-am," he said, I really must go and shower!" And taking her hand gently, he kissed it. Tissie melted on the spot, giving a girlish giggle.

My God! I thought incredulously, the old girl fancies him!

***

I lead him along the corridor shaking my head in disbelief. With a backward glance, I motioned him to keep up, not making any allowances for his two huge suitcases. He looked strong enough to cope.

"Sorry, no lift," I said unsmiling. "You'll have to put up with our primitive ways." He looked confused, then after a few seconds delay, his brain leapt the language barrier.

"Ah, now I understand, no elevator."

"It's called a lift here," I said, still angry with him for embarrassing me. "This is England. You'll have to get used to it." He shrugged and hoisted the suitcases higher, quickening his step to follow. If I seemed calm and demure on the outside, it certainly was not the reality.

He was good looking, strikingly so. At around six feet, with dark, curly, close-cropped hair he would stand out in any crowd. The fine bone structure of his face set him apart from the 'also-rans', with the brooding looks of James Dean and the athletic body of a young Patrick Swayze. His tight trousers left little to the imagination either. It was little wonder that Tissue was simpering.

He reminded me of a magnificent racehorse at the very peak of its career. Had it been possible to see a cross-section of him, there would probably have been the word 'thoroughbred' written all the way through. Why then, did the close proximity of him make me feel strange, in a way that was not pleasurable but disturbing?

As we started to climb the staircase, a sharp tingling, just behind my left ear caught me by surprise, my fingers instinctively going to the spot. In a frenzy of sudden dizziness, I clutched at the bannister-rail with my free hand, as the staircase seemed to sway underfoot.

As a teenager, I had become used to this sensation when 'spirit people' came close and I had learned to live with it, but this was different and for a few seconds, it hurt. In that short space of time, I knew it was a warning. Even when I had chosen to ignore my voices, I quickly learned from experience that some things only went away if I paid heed to them; a bit like the gas and electric bills!

If the 'spirit people thought something of sufficient importance for either my development or safety, then they would nag me until I did it and it was usually the right decision. It was nevertheless my decision whether I listened or not, but on this occasion, it seemed that someone was pretty keen to focus my attention.

Do not get close to this man and if you do not pay heed you will suffer for it!

***

Not daring to look around in case he saw, I took a deep breath. Something strange was happening, Hold on, I'm a big girl now! I countered, and suddenly a cacophony of noise seemed to fill my head, a thousand voices all repeating the same word, Listenlistenlistenlistenlistenlistenlistenlistenlistenlistenlistenlisten listenlistenlisten.

something to be feared, and something that lurked in the unlit corners of a dingy room, making me listen. Never before had I experienced anything so dark and threatening.

Why have you come here, Robbie? Disturbing the natural balance of things, for no good will ever come of it. You are going to hurt me.

I was sure of it!

"You okay, Ma-am?" His voice broke the mood, sharply, suddenly severing a link and all was silent again, comfort returning as quickly, the stairs feeling solid under my feet once more.

"Of course, I am," I said softly, breathing hard. "Thank you."

After all, it was no big deal. I had been attracted to men before; in love even, several times or so I thought. It had been the intense, desperate experimenting love of the early teenage years, when every occasion was 'IT', 'The Real Thing', except, of course, it wasn't. Matthew and I hadn't survived the first six months of my Nurse Training; the demands of the job had been so great.

These were the so-called 'swinging '60s', but we really did not sleep around. There was still the stigma of bringing shame on the family and anyway, I was much too frightened of my Father! The Pill had only just become widely available, but sexually liberating? Most probably for some, but there was also a lot of hype.

So often I've heard the quote, "If you can't remember the 60's, then you weren't there." Well, I definitely was there and it was a great time to grow up, but the 'free love' reputation has been outrageously embroidered over the decades. It was actually quite an effort to live up to the expectation of what the media told us we were doing, whether we were or not.

Student nurses were (and still are) infamous for playing hard, but unfortunately hadn't a great deal of time to do it!

I lead Robbie up to the second floor, walking slowly and deliberately, the melancholy mood broken, amused and smiling to myself now, ignoring the gasps and stares, as nurses seemed to appear en masse from nowhere. Dozens of pairs of eyes watched as, with no apparent shame, Paola Green led a man up the stairs to her room in full view of Tissie!

After what seemed the longest walk of my life, we reached the door of his room, the one next to mine. I was myself again, though still a little angry with him.

"Why did you deliberately embarrass me in there?" I demanded.

He grinned broadly, the dark brown eyes soft as butter.

"You blush so beautifully, only true English roses do that." My eyes narrowed at his audacity, not yet ready for compliments from this brash American.

"Oh, I would be careful of roses if I were you," I said, raising an eyebrow, "They have very sharp thorns."

"Touché, Ma-am!" He smiled again, this time a much gentler smile.

"My name is Paola," I said. "May I ask you something rather personal?"

"Why sure you can, Ma-am, errr… sorry, Paola." He held up his hands in a submissive gesture. In turn, I held up my hand, posing the wrist to drop limply.

"Are you…? Well, you know!"

It was his turn to blush.

"I certainly am not!"

"Then if you want a bit of advice," I said pointing to the crowd of young women staring open-mouthed, "I'd lock my door tonight if I were you."

"Touché again," he said and with a final smile that made my knees weaken, closed and locked the door with a loud click.

Chapter Six

Despite it being rather late, I did not feel at all like sleep. Sitting in front of the mirror, I brushed my hair and stared at the young woman looking back at me. I stuck out my tongue and made a face.

What an exhausting day! I thought, I should be completely worn out so why aren't I?

I lay on the bed and recalled the events of the last couple of days, smirking and ashamed that it never occurred to me that the cat might be 'expecting'. It would take a long time to live that one down.

Then there was Robbie. What about him?

A good-looking American guy, sleeping not ten feet away in the adjoining room and given to me to look after personally, by Tissie. Maybe, we would have to rename the 'Virgins' retreat', as the Nurses' Home was affectionately known.

I should have been ecstatic; the envy of every young woman who lived there, but the whole situation, though a 'first' didn't seem quite right somehow. Young women together, behave as young women tend to in the absence of men, letting their hair down and doing the girlie things in which men have no right to play a part. It was cosy and comfortable, with no need to consider modesty or manners. I feared that our safe, pleasant haven, of tights on the radiators and sanitary towel machines in the toilets, would now have to be changed. Would any of us feel quite so comfortable from now on? A man moving in changed the status of the place. Would he become the cat amongst our pigeons, the fox in our hen house, a fly in our ointment? I was certain that all our lives were about to change and feared that it would be not for the better.

***

In the warmth of my little room, I was beginning to relax, the first ripples of sleepiness making my eyelids heavy, as I slipped gently between the deliciously soft sheets and dozed.

Suddenly, a light burst, somewhere in my head, jolting me back to full consciousness. Jumping violently, as though I had touched a live wire, I sat up. From somewhere behind my ear, came whispered voices.

Hoping that it was not another episode like the one on the stairs, I took a deep breath and allowed myself to relax, the way I had learned over the years.

The jumbled whisperings continued for a few seconds gradually clearing, until only one remained. It was the familiar voice of an old lady I had come to know.

I called her Edith and many years ago she had attached herself to me and had become one of my guides. Whether or not that had been her name I don't know, but she had never corrected me, but I had always felt safe with her, though only ever hearing her voice.

She had first come when I was about fifteen, at first wondering if she had been a relative; having some romantic notion that perhaps she had been my great-grandmother or someone like that. She had never enlightened me despite my asking, so maybe it was one of those things I wasn't supposed to know. Anyway, she felt like a 'granny' influence and that was enough and I was satisfied with that. She was my guardian, the one I spoke to in times of trouble and I knew I was safe if she was around.

She brought with her the smell of lavender, which lingered in my room for hours afterwards. Often, I smelled the flowers long before she came, but not tonight.

"Paola," she whispered, "we haven't spoken for a while."

With my eyes closed, I felt her presence, so near as to feel her soft breath, warm against my cheek, mingled with lavender and warm fresh-baked scones.

So much seems to have happened lately. I allowed my thoughts to reach out and mingle with hers.

"I know, child." Her words were clear. "These next few months will bring a big change in your life. You will begin to understand so much better."

Understand what? I asked silently. She didn't answer straight away, but I knew she was still there.

"The time is right for you to move forward," she said at last, "but all you feel right now is disturbance. Have faith, it will all come right if you allow it too."

The last few words drifted away and she was gone as suddenly as she had come. I was nonplussed, as so frequently happened at these times. It seemed that tantalising snippets of information were given and I had to work it out for myself, at times exasperating. My demands for precise information were always met with silence.

Patience was not my strong point and I often had to remind myself of the promise I made to listen. It was obviously a part of the learning process, teaching me patience.

I got up from the bed, annoyingly wide-awake now and went down to the kitchen, to make cocoa. Sitting by the boiler in the huge empty kitchen, I finally began to feel sleepy again and so taking the remains of the drink with me returned to my room and slept.

***

When I woke, dawn had broken. I felt terrible, shaking with cold, my head throbbing as, huddling beneath the blankets I tried in vain to keep warm. Even a hot water bottle filled from the hot tap didn't help much, as the water was never very warm at this hour. With chattering teeth, I pulled on a cardigan, dressing gown and socks, but that didn't help much either. I knew I had a fever and my face was burning hot.

It always seems so unfair that when you have a high temperature, all your instincts tell you to wrap up because you are freezing. Of course, this is the worst thing you can do. What you need, is to cool down, then you will feel better. I never met anyone yet who didn't take a very dim view of someone taking the blankets away when they were actually shivering with cold.

I lay beneath the blankets shaking and trying in vain to sleep, until the insistent ringing of the alarm clock sent me struggling down to breakfast.

I slumped down heavily into a chair, hardly able to hold up my head, an entire corps of drums beating a tattoo inside it.

"Just coffee thanks, Mary," I said, acknowledging our maid. "I really don't feel like eating this morning."

There was no such thing as having to trudge over to the Staff Dining room in the main hospital where everyone took meals whilst on duty. We ate in comparative luxury in the Nurses' Home, at properly set tables with good cutlery, crockery and fresh linen napkins.

From the next table, Tissie looked up sharply and frowned. Missing breakfast was unacceptable as far as she was concerned and from the look she gave me, quite high on her list of rules.

"My girls need a good start to the day," she was often heard to proclaim. "How can you possibly expect to do a good day's work on an empty stomach?" She turned to face me and caught sight of my pale face. "Oh, good grief girl, whatever is the matter with you?" Painfully I raised my head, my stinging eyes half-open.

"I think I have the 'Flu or something," I said hoarsely, "Coffee's all I'd better have."

She rose; arms outstretched like an avenging angel and placed a cool hand on my forehead.

"You will not my girl!" she retorted, already marching me back up the stairs. "It's back to bed for you this minute. I'll have Mary bring you up some food and fruit juice in a little while."

There was no point in arguing with Tissie when she was in full flow, even if I had felt like it.

Scuttling round my room like a whirlwind, she quickly changed the sheets, (probably breaking the three-minute record by miles,) as I looked on passively, propped up in a corner and hanging on to the sink for support. As she ushered me into bed, I briefly opened my mouth to thank her, only to be silenced as a thermometer was unceremoniously inserted in it.

"Goodness me!" she exclaimed, "one hundred and four degrees! Now you are to stay in that bed and don't get up until I tell you." She headed for the door and turned. "And above all don't go worrying your head about that wretched cat. It's getting treated better than Royalty." I managed a weak smile, as she sailed out to administer to some other poor sick soul, whether they wanted it or not. Seconds before I lapsed into sleep, I thought, that behind that guise of ferocity beat a heart of pure gold. We were 'her girls', her only family and she loved us all as her own, even though it was a trifle hard to believe sometimes.

I was walking in a familiar place where I had spent so many long summer days. It was a balmy afternoon and the sky was cornflower blue with fluffy white clouds far into the distance. The place was called 'High Meadow', because that was just what it was. The field on one side of the path sloped gently down to a stream at the bottom and on the other side, the panoramic view of the village where I was born. It was a breathtaking place where the earth met with the sky, in that perfect harmony one only usually finds on an artist's canvas. On a day such as this, it was the most perfect place on earth.

We would come here after school, my childhood friends and I, bringing picnic teas. There was no need for adult supervision. This was the late fifties and kids could still play safely in our little village where everybody knew everyone else; an expectation of safety that has long since vanished. The age of innocence seems to get less with each passing year. Unfortunately, we dare not give our children the same freedom to explore and develop their spirit of adventure, as we did. We, as parents have become too afraid to allow them the necessary independence to discover the wonderment in the world. We dare not expose them to the evil which lurks out there, unseen and not always obvious. Somehow, whilst trying to protect, we have lost sight of something vitally important. Children need freedom to grow; physically, mentally, socially and spiritually. Risks are everywhere and living your life is the biggest risk of all. We must somehow find a way to balance that risk.

Of course, we were told not to speak to strangers, or to take sweets from anyone, but in fact, there were few strangers. Children could go out into the village and its surroundings, without their parents being scared to death, the moment they were out of sight.

'High Meadow' was an accepted place where children played, as was the park and down by the stream; the bigger children taking care of the little ones.

I knew by name, all the wildflowers that grew in profusion in the lush meadow. There was 'egg and bacon', (purple and yellow vetch) buttercups, daisies, field yarrow (which smelled bitter) and purple and white clover. If you pulled out the clover petals and sucked them, they tasted sweet; this, of course, was before the blanket use of pesticides.

Further down the boggy slope to the river, grew stately 'ladies smock' and 'shepherd's purse'.

We would spend hours trying to 'dam' the river, which was little more than a gentle stream, splashing and paddling, shoes and socks discarded on the bank.

The boys, with their jam jars, would catch 'sticklebacks', whilst water voles swam up and down unconcerned, going about their business. Further downstream, where the trees overhung the river, there was shade on hot days to snooze and cool off, our toes dabbling in the water and if you were very still and quiet, the kingfishers would perch near the bank on an overhanging branch.

Suddenly a flash of translucent blue would dive into the river making hardly a ripple, before returning with a struggling fish in its beak. The little bird then proceeded to bang the fish repeatedly on the branch, before swallowing the poor thing whole, and diving in for another. It truly was an idyllic place for any child to grow up. I felt very lucky.

Today, however, I was walking through 'High Meadow', not as a child, but an adult, evocative memories instantly returning. Small blue butterflies fluttered around my feet amongst the harebells and clover as I walked along the dusty path. With the warm sun on my face, it was wonderful to engage in such a simple pleasure once more.

It was then that I saw her, a little way ahead of me, face upturned to catch the rays of the sun. Linnie! It was Linnie. Her beautiful hair cascaded down her back, gently swishing to and fro, caught by the gentle breeze as she sat in the long grass. I began to run toward her, my jaw dropping in wonder, the scent of a long-forgotten perfume filling my nostrils; 'Blue Grass!'

"Linnie. It's you!"

She didn't seem to hear me and I called again, louder this time. She bent forward to pick a bunch of clover and buttercups, sniffing at them as she rose from the grass.

"Linnie! It's me!" I cried louder still, "don't go."

She turned for a moment to look in my direction, then smiling sadly began to walk away, head bent forward.

I ran after her, determined not to let her go again. There were so many things I needed to ask; so much I needed to say, to tell her. But, no matter how fast I ran, I got no closer, the distance between us stayed the same. My legs felt like lead as she reached the stile and passed effortlessly between the munching cows and down into the next field and I knew I mustn't follow.

Then as I watched sadly, breathlessly, she was gone.

***

I woke in a terrible panic, damp with perspiration, heart hammering in my chest. I drank some orange juice, fell back on the pillows and was aware of nothing once more. Rousing from feverish slumber from time to time, either intolerably hot or cold and shivering, I was not really aware of anything around me. From time to time, there seemed to be someone in the room, but felt too ill to even open my eyes. Sometimes I woke with a tremendous start, as after a nightmare, vivid for only a few seconds, before slipping into oblivion again.

Then, quite suddenly, it was daylight. The sun was streaming in through the window, the fever gone. I felt better, though a bit weak and wobbly, but above all, I was hungry.

Washing my face and combing my hair quickly, I put on a dressing gown and went downstairs in search of food. At the foot of the staircase, I met Tissie.

"Oh, at last," she said, "you are feeling better I see. Are you ready for that meal now?"

"Yes please," I said, "Did I sleep for long?"

"Well, let's put it like this," said Tissie smiling and folding her arms across her ample chest, "I think breakfast may be a bit cold now. After all, you have been 'missing' for three days!"

I had lost three whole days and nights of my life, a really strange feeling!

"You have been quite ill my dear child," Tissie said, arms still folded. "We were quite worried about you. By the way, who is Lynn? Is she your sister?"

"No," I said, "a good friend," not wanting to explain further.

"You were a bit delirious and calling for her a good deal. Oh, by the way, I nearly forgot, you were so restless, that you knocked your alarm clock off the bedside table. I'm afraid it's well and truly broken."

I thanked her and groaned inwardly. I was hopeless at getting up in the mornings, even with a bell ringing in my ear.

As she turned to go, I quickly took a couple of steps after her, touching her sleeve gently and she turned enquiringly.

"Thank you for taking care of me," I said, a bit embarrassed.

She tossed her head and was her prim and proper self once more.

"Nothing to do with me!" she exclaimed briskly. "Nature will always heal if it's allowed to."

"Well thank you anyway," I said.

She gave me a curt nod, but I detected, just for a second, a ghost of a smile in her eyes.

It was Tissie in my room when I briefly woke, I was sure of it. It was she who had looked after me and brought drinks. I bet she had barely taken her eyes off me for three days and nights. I wanted to show my gratitude, but she clearly wasn't used to being thanked. Maybe she had felt it was her duty, but deep down I knew her feelings for us ran much deeper than that. From that day I kept a special place in my heart for her too.

***

With a good breakfast inside me, I recovered with a speed that only the young and fit can and by the next day, was completely back to normal.

It was my weekend off, so I went home to catch up on all the news. Mother's hair had not become any greyer since I last saw her and Dad and still sane, so it could be assumed that Annie's musical talents on the violin were improving. The dog ignored me completely, as if unable to forgive me for deserting the sinking ship.

It was late evening when I returned to the Nurses' Home. The nights were 'drawing in', getting darker and colder. Winter would soon to be here and yet another summer would only be a distant memory.

In the Nurses' Home, my side of the building was already carried an 'Icelandic' chill. It was time to get out my wincyette pyjamas and big furry slippers, which were reserved for winter nights. One had to keep warm in that draughty old building, especially after being ill.

Later I sat in the kitchen, by the Aga, drinking a mug of cocoa and feeling sleepy, when a sudden thought struck me.

Oh, hell! The clock. I had meant to ask Mum if she would lend me the spare. How on earth was I going to wake up for early shift without one? I was hopeless at getting up!

The door opened, interrupting the moment of panic and Robbie came in, suitably muffled up for winter. He seemed pleased to see me and I was genuinely pleased to see him.

"Well Hi there," he said raising his eyebrows, "Back in the land of the living so I see. Are you feeling better?" He warmed his hands on the front of the Aga.

"Much, thank you," I replied. "Are you settling in alright?"

"Yeah," he nodded, screwing up his nose. "Been to a movie by myself. The 'pictures' I think you call it here, Yeah?" See, I'm beginning to understand your quaint language already."

"Yeah!" I mimicked him, smiling. He was looking at my big furry slippers with some amusement.

"Did you shoot them yourself," he asked, pointing to them.

"Would you like some cocoa?" I asked.

"What the hell is cocoa? He was still fascinated by the slippers.

"Ah," I would have to translate. "I think you call it chocolate."

I was beginning to like this brash American.

"In that case then," he said with a nod of his head, "if it's no bother, I'd love some."

I rose and busied myself with the milk, though even with my back to him, I knew he was watching me.

"A favour for a favour then." I ventured, handing him the steaming mug.

"You just name it, honey," he said, his eyes still fixed on my slippers, probably wondering what sort of animal they had come from originally and so I continued despite not having his full attention.

I'm back at work tomorrow morning." I said. "Will you knock me up at around six am?" His eyes widened like saucers and he stared, the mug halfway to his lips.

"Will I what?" The words came out as a strangled squeak.

"I broke my alarm clock. I was wondering if you would mind knocking me up at six o'clock? That's if it's no trouble." His mouth gaped, eyes almost popping out.

"If it's no…" he began. "Look, are you sure about this? It's a helluva way to be woken up."

"Oh, just bang on my door about six," I said. "It'll be alright."

"Are you completely sure about this?" he said, looking at me curiously.

"Oh, I'll never get up otherwise."

Robbie shook his head; his face breaking into a broad grin, as though suddenly all his dreams had come true. He stood looking at me inanely for a few seconds.

"I was told that English women were very reserved about that sort of thing!" he exclaimed. "But I gotta tell ya'. Wow Pao!" He took a few steps towards me, holding out his arms. "Wow Pao!" he repeated breathlessly.

Anticipating an impending hug, I took a quick step back to escape, only to find myself pressed against the wall.

"What is the matter with you for Heaven's sake?" I cried indignantly, fending him off with both arms. "Look I told you, I broke my clock. It's no big deal. If you don't want to do it, I can always ask someone else. And another thing… Don't call me Pao! It sounds like something out of a Batman comic. Wowwee! Zap! Pow!"

Robbie put his head on one side and regarded me curiously.

"My name is PA-O-LA," I said, spelling it out, as if to a small child. "Watch my lips!"

"Oh, honey, I was!" Suddenly he stopped, smirked and held up his hands, a chink of realisation dawning. "Wait a minute."

He started to laugh, at first, merely a chuckle, which exploded as he lost control, until he was all but rolling on the floor, clutching his sides. I stood and stared, convinced that I was in the kitchen late at night with a maniac. He looked up at me from time to time as the convulsions of mirth died down, until finally, he was able to speak.

"Sit down a moment, please," he said, wiping the tears from his eyes. I sat, bewildered, eyebrows raised enquiringly.

His face contorted with mirth again, fighting to regain composure, lips trembling. Like Queen Victoria, I was not amused.

"You know this conversation we just had?" I nodded not looking at him.

"Well," he said, "I think perhaps I'd better explain."

There followed the most excruciatingly embarrassing few minutes I have ever spent as Robbie tried valiantly, between guffaws, to explain that the expression 'to be knocked up' had a completely different meaning in the good old United States of America!

Red-faced and wishing the ground would open up and swallow me, I tried to make a dignified exit from the kitchen, unsuccessfully.

The poor man had only been in our country a few days and he had already been propositioned by a convalescing nymphomaniac, wearing wincyette pyjamas and furry slippers. My suffering was compounded, by his miserable attempt to keep a straight face. How I hated this brash American!

Without further ado, I fled from the kitchen and up the stairs, vowing to buy a new alarm clock the very next day.

I did lock the door of my room however, just in case.

Chapter Seven

I studiously avoided Robbie for the next few days. The mere thought of our last conversation was enough to cause my colour to rise rapidly.

When he had tapped on my door the following morning at six and enquired if I was awake, I had answered with a very curt, "Yes thank you!" However, it seemed that fate was hell-bent on throwing us together, whether I liked it or not.

We had both been assigned to the children's ward. It was called the Princess Margaret Unit or Maggie's as someone had christened it long before my time. It was situated right at the top of the main hospital building, up six flights of stairs, should the lift not be working, which all too frequently it wasn't.

It was named after the Queen's sister, who had come to open it whilst she was a mere child herself.

It consisted of two wards built along the 'long corridor' design with rooms off and the Sister's office in the middle, so she was able to see what was happening. At either end were rooms with huge doors, which opened onto a balcony. Those rather spacious rooms afforded parents the luxury of being able to stay with their sick child, although they had to sleep in a chair at the side of the bed.

Today, it is hard to imagine leaving children at times when they need their parents the most, but we weren't half so enlightened then. It was feared that parents might interfere with the smooth running of the ward, or worse still, that they might usurp Sister's authority by actually asking for some involvement in their own child's care. What a long way we have all come, thank goodness and not before time.

Even if I did find myself working alongside the man responsible for the most acutely embarrassing moment of my life so far, it proved to be a lovely change. Such a far cry, from all those old men, suffering out their last weeks on this earth.

Suddenly we were surrounded by much younger lives, though equally as mischievous and troublesome in some cases, but full to the brim with life and energy.

Some were ill; of course; they wouldn't have been there otherwise, but for the majority of the time it was a place of happy sounds and few tragedies.

It was a place of tiny sandwiches minus their crusts, which little fingers could easily manage, and of sticky sweets and treats. There were games to play, bedtime stories to read and best of all, unlimited cuddles for all that wanted them and I was in Heaven. But it was the babies that gave me the most joy and I used to make up any excuse to sneak off and hold them. If I didn't come to Sister's call, she always knew where to find me.

Being the start of winter, the babies and toddlers had started to be admitted with chest infections and particularly Bronchitis. The hospital was situated in the middle of town in an area of low employment and social deprivation.

On the outskirts of the town were lots of Victorian 'back-to-back' terraces, with very narrow streets between; no real gardens, merely a backyard. Very few homes had central heating in those days and many were damp. Poor families often hadn't the money to feed their children properly and with large families living in overcrowded conditions, infections ran riot. Croup and whooping cough were common in winter amongst the under-fives, but it was often poor home circumstances that brought them into the hospital.

The little children were nursed in steam tents to 'loosen their chests'. It was really a big plastic bubble thrown over the cot, into which was fed a steaming kettle with a long spout. In the kettle with the water was mixed Tinc. Benz Co Meth. (Friar's Balsam) with its pungent and instantly recognisable smell.

As with the geriatric wards, it was obvious where you were working, as the smell clung to your clothes and hair, but as smells go it was a distinct improvement.

Caring for these little ones was a pleasure. They got better quite quickly and it was satisfying that something so simple could make such a difference. It was not unusual, however, for the same child to be admitted four or five times over the space of the winter. As soon as they returned home the whole cycle of damp houses and poor diet would begin again, until inevitably the child caught a cold which went to its chest and in they would come again.

We were powerless to treat the cause, wages were poor in the area and large families were still the norm. It was frustrating that the best we could do were to treat the consequences.

I loved working on that ward and caring for those tiny children with their poorly chests, even though there was a penalty to be paid.

The nurse who looked after them also had the dubious privilege of cleaning the steam kettles. The awful task had to be done every three days, or the brown sticky Tinc. Benz would set solid in the kettles, rendering them useless. The hours I spent chipping away at the things in order to earn the right to cuddle those babies!

First of all, the insides of the kettles had to be soaked in boiling water to soften the toffee-like mess inside. Then they had to be rinsed out with alcohol and the whole contraption shaken vigorously before the silt was poured down the sluice and they were heavy!

On that particular day, Robbie had offered to help me with the job. I was deeply suspicious of his motives at first, sincere though he seemed. He was probably trying to get back into my good books and raise my opinion of him. I decided to accept his offer whilst thinking of another way to make him suffer. He was not getting away with it as easily as that. However, if it meant help with so terrible a job, I felt it worth a temporary truce. It took two people to lift the things anyhow.

It was me who struck up a conversation as we busied ourselves.

"So then, Robbie, where in America are you from?" I ventured.

"Texas, the lone star state," he replied proudly.

"Whereabouts is that then? I enquired. He looked at me incredulously.

"Really Paola, didn't you take geography at college then?" I didn't answer. He looked at me, folded his arms and leaned on the wall.

"Well Ma'am," he began, "let me explain. You go right outta' this building and make a right. Keep on going until you get to the ocean, then go all the way over and when you see Liberty, give her a cheery wave and turn left. When you get to South Carolina make another left through Tennessee and Arkansas. Are you with me so far honey?"

My eyes narrowed peevishly. God! He was insufferable.

"Hold it, don't hit me yet Ma'am we're nearly there," he went on quickly before I could think of a suitable reply. "You'll come to Dallas and even you must remember Dallas! You are now in Texas. Well about a hundred miles the other side, that's where I come from. If you hit the Mexican border you've gone too far."

I sighed deeply. Why was it that all Yanks thought they were so smart? Did he think I was a country bumpkin or something? This brash American was once again beginning to get on my nerves. I put down my cleaning cloth, walked over to him, leaned on the same wall and folded my arms.

"Actually," I said, "I believe that from 1836 to 1845 Texas was an independent nation in its own right and goes eight hundred miles from east to west and one thousand miles from top to bottom." He turned to look at me, his jaw-dropping open, but I didn't give him chance to speak. "Regional differences I believe, are vast, from swampy east to tropical Gulf Coast, with a melting-pot of cultures. It is said that Texans are welcoming and friendly, so I think that particular trait must have missed a generation with you, eh honey, you still with me by the way? So, pardon me, cowboy," I said with a mock touch of an invisible Stetson, "just get back on your horse and bugger off into the sunset."

He closed his mouth and held up his hands in a submissive gesture, shaking his head.

"God!" he said quietly, "I guess I really deserved that. Sorry Pao, I mean Paola, Oh, God, sorry, sorry, sorry… what sort of a name is Paola anyway, are your folks Italian?"

"Actually," I said, really enjoying his discomfort and still miffed, "I should have been called Paula, after the landlady at the local pub. My dad had been in there celebrating yet another daughter and was drunk when he went to register my birth.

He spelt it wrong and I was stuck with it." Our eyes met we both fell about laughing. The score was now one each and all was forgiven.

***

Two weeks later Robbie and I were scheduled to do our first block of night duty together.

This experience opened up a whole new existence and you either loved it or hated it. I loved it, even though sleeping in the daytime did take a bit of getting used to. Your body clock is thrown out of synchronisation and then is expected to return to normal a week later during your four nights off.

Digestion is the first thing to suffer, as you go to bed, after eating breakfast only to wake up and have dinner. No wonder we all suffered from indigestion and worse still, flatulence.

Depending on which ward you happened to be on, the nights could be either deadly quiet or hellishly busy. Quiet was worse, a twelve-hour shift was a very long time if there was not much to do.

The children's ward was always a hive of activity day or night. Babies needed feeding all night long and we made all our own feeds up in those days (no pre-pack) in the little 'milk kitchen' which had to be kept scrupulously clean at all times and cleaning was a big part of a nurse's duties. If you had a spare moment, it was spent scrubbing everything from lockers to trolley wheels. The ward had its own cleaner, but all she seemed to do was constantly wash and buff the floors, which incidentally, you could almost see your face in.

As any parent knows, sick children do not sleep well, especially when in unfamiliar surroundings.

I was making feeds up in the kitchen one night, alone and content with my lot. This, I decided was where I belonged, my vocation in life and vowed one day to have lots of children of my own, if the day ever came when I found my handsome prince.

There is always the exception, which proves the rule and the weather had been unusually mild, which meant that there were less sick children and those who were on the ward were all sleeping peacefully. In the early hours, Robbie and I had the chance to talk, this time a much friendlier and mature conversation.

He had indeed been born and brought up in Texas and it was clear that he loved the place, for whenever home was mentioned, a smile came, which quickly spread to his eyes. He came from a good family, where money had never been in short supply; his Father a surgeon, his Mother, a lawyer. They owned a fair size ranch house, just far enough away from the nearest city for Robbie to class himself as a country boy, but close enough to 'go into town and have fun!' His Father had bought a battered old 'Chevy' for him and his three brothers to share. In spite of a good income, the kids clearly weren't spoilt.

My only experience of Americans came from the cinema, where 'rich kids', were often portrayed as spoiled and badly behaved. Or the gun-toting cowboys of 'spaghetti westerns' and quite frankly I felt it didn't do the national image any favours. I was glad Robbie seemed quite ordinary.

His brothers were younger, eighteen months separating each sibling and he was close to them, as he was to his parents. They seemed to be a happy family, with well-adjusted kids. Robbie showed me lots of family photographs of them all, camping, fishing and riding, on vacations to the coast and the wild countryside.

As we talked, relaxed in each other's company now, I got the impression that great things were expected of him, nevertheless. He explained to me the American system of schooling, rather different from ours, which seemed much more 'laid back'. It was committed to turning out the academically bright in their thousands, but it seemed to me, lacking for those who didn't quite make the grade.

Sport was an important part of the curriculum, here in the fifties and sixties, much more so than today. It is a real travesty that it has taken four decades to realise that the health of future generations could be favourably influenced by a few hours of compulsory exercise every week. We used to complain bitterly about those cross-country runs in the rain and snow, hockey practice until our knees were blue with cold and PE in the school gym, but we had cause to be grateful later on in life for the basic level of fitness it gave us.

I'm not so sure that is the case today, when you look around and see the obesity in our streets and early deaths from cardiovascular disease.

If sport played a large role here in Britain, then in the States, it was huge. Participation was expected of everyone, woven into the fabric of everyday life and it was big business. All the family joined in too, which was probably the main difference between our countries.

Here in Britain, football was male-dominated and it was the boys who got to go to matches. Very few women were seen in football grounds then. Good grief! Ladies toilets weren't even provided at some stadiums until the 1980s! What sort of a message did that send out?

American football stadiums were purpose-built, family-orientated places with many more comforts to ensure the family's enjoyment of the whole experience. Maybe these factors were responsible for the difference in the way we viewed our participation in sport.

It became clear that Robbie's sporting love was baseball, which I, much to his annoyance referred to as 'rounders on a bigger scale'. He would wax lyrical for hours on the finer points of the game, which I could barely grasp, and he spoke about some of the players in reverential hushed tones.

"One day," he promised, "I'll take you to a game and you'll be hooked. Then you'll understand what it's all about." I smiled indulgently; failing to comprehend how a grown man could get so excited over a game of 'rounders'.

He began to get cross with me when I voiced my disgust, at any country where the greatest ambition for a girl, seemed that of becoming a cheerleader. I knew that he was a bit of a chauvinist and I wondered if he had been used to women with strong opinions of their own.

I might have come from a family of five women, but Father always instilled into us, that we were as 'good as any man', if we put our minds to it. Not only were we taught to cook, sew and polish, but also how to mend a puncture, a bit of bricklaying and emergency plumbing if required. Dad saw to that.

I had read an article in the early sixties, written in America, which instructed young brides that the only skills needed to snare and keep a husband happy, was the ability to bake a pie and cook a good steak and was totally incensed at the time.

I felt well equipped to challenge Robbie about his own attitude to women.

"So then, Robbie," I began, leaning back in my chair, "what do you think of women?"

"I don't believe they should all be cheerleaders," he replied cautiously. "After all what would we do for waitresses?" I shot upright ready for the challenge.

Was he goading me? "Oh, and I suppose you think we should be kept pregnant, barefoot and in the kitchen?"

"Not at all, Ma-am!" he exclaimed defensively and as usual reverting to formality when challenged. "I believe that no-one should be made to do anything they don't want to do. Anyway, what do you want to be, Prime Minister I suppose?" He was mocking me now, adopting a 'Nah-nah-nee-nah-nah' voice.

"Hey, hold on there," I said, "And why not? I'll bet you it won't be too many years before we have a woman Prime Minister."

"Now you are being ridiculous," he said laughing out loud.

His attitude intrigued me. I was sure of one thing. There was much more to this American than met the eye and I found myself thinking about him more than was good for me. He was capable of being utterly charming and then the next moment so infuriating that I wanted to kill him. He could shift between one persona and the next, with little effort. I was determined to find out what made him tick, one way or another.

There was something else about Robbie though, something he probably wasn't aware of himself and that was a hint of conflict behind those dark brown eyes. I had seen it on a few occasions when he had been deep in thought and hadn't been aware of me watching. I desperately wanted to know what it was; I had a pressing need to find out.

"Steady," a voice had whispered, behind my ear, "maybe this is one thing you should not pursue. Think very carefully." The words were not delivered with any real conviction. Maybe on this occasion, it had been accepted that I was not going to listen, despite all advice to the contrary.

What do I really know about you, Robbie? I asked myself the next night, as I lay sleeplessly in bed. Do I really like you enough to care? I was rather afraid I did.

Oh, no Paola, not now! You have far too much revising to concentrate on without the distraction of a man. Don't you dare allow yourself to fall for him.

"Absolutely," whispered a soft but firm voice behind my ear, "now get some sleep or you won't be fit for anything!"

It was the first of four nights off and my body clock was not adjusting well.

I should be sleeping; I remonstrated with myself, not lying here after midnight trying to analyse the vagaries of male behaviour.

There was no sound from the adjoining room. The rest of the building was quiet save for the occasional creaks and moans of the ancient central heating pipes.

Most likely been asleep for hours, I thought, dreaming of Texas and those bloody empty-headed cheerleaders!

I knew he had been to medical school and it was there, something had happened that was significant enough to make him take a year off and leave the country. I wondered what it was, that was serious enough to make him do that? Had he made some awful mistake? No, surely medical students didn't get near enough to patients to do any real damage? After all, it was America, not England.

I thought it more likely that he'd done some lasting and increasingly obvious 'damage' to the Principle's daughter and had to make himself scarce for a while.

For Robbie had the morals of a sewer rat!

His greatest weakness was women, completely unable to resist pretty girls, but not just any; they had to have a certain look; smaller than him, which wasn't difficult, intelligent, slim and with a perfect complexion. He preferred brunettes with long flowing hair and fine bone structure.

When I went out into town, I used to play a little game, which involved looking at women in the street and mentally awarding them a ratio of probability; i.e. how 'Robbiesque' they were. It became quite a hobby, but I had to stop when folk started giving me funny looks and anyway it seemed a bit like 'pimping'.

The fact of the matter was that Robbie was awfully good-looking. It seemed he only had to smile at a girl and she would follow him home. He never had a problem getting them into the Nurses' Home and how the hell he did it no-one knew. I suppose that a woman wouldn't have looked out of place there. The majority of British girls had never met an American, so that was probably a big attraction too.

I bet he couldn't believe his luck when he was given a room in the 'home'. I was incredulous at Tissie's unwavering trust. It was like giving a starving fox the free run of a poultry farm! If only she had known what he was like, the poor old dear would have had a heart attack.

Robbie's idea of safe sex was making sure the old girl was safely tucked up in bed before he went into action, deftly leading girls on tiptoe past her room and upstairs. If there were any danger that Tissie was still up and about, he would lead them in through a tiny basement door at the back of the boiler house; no doubt holding them very close with the threat of spiders.

During those first few months, he methodically worked his way through all the nurses on the first floor and halfway across the second, not to mention assorted acquaintances brought in from outside the hospital. He was not in the least ashamed or embarrassed when any of us caught him showing a girl into his room either, openly acknowledging his weakness, he was neither going to apologize for it or fight it.

Robbie referred to his 'lady friends' as his 'achievements'. He went through women so quickly, I wondered how he managed to keep them all apart and stop them from clawing each other's eyes out. How on earth he remembered all their names, one could only marvel. Each encounter lasted a mere few days, at the most a week, then he was off to the next one like a demented bee in search of another flower.

I thought that night duty might cramp his style and for a short time, it did. We worked twelve-hour shifts, ten nights on and four nights off. He would have been superhuman to keep up the pace; not that he didn't have a damn good try.

Where did he find the energy after a long stretch of night duty? He sure packed a lot of living into those few short days and nights off.

It was the first of our nights off and I was exhausted. I don't think I could have stood on my feet for another twelve hours, so on the dot of nine p.m. I fell into bed and this, after a full day's sleep.

By one-thirty a.m. I hadn't closed my eyes. By two a.m. I could stand it no longer, even with my head underneath two pillows it didn't dull the noise.

Angrily kicking back the covers, I jumped out of bed.

"Oh, Robbie!" came moaning cries of female passion through the wall, "Robbie, Robbie!"

"Oh, God," I moaned too, but not for the same reason. "He's bloody well at it again." Violently I drummed my fists on the adjoining wall.

"Robbie, you sod, listen to me! For God's sake hurry up and get on with it, so we can all get some flamin' sleep will you?" I gave the wall a final thump for added effect.

There was a shriek followed by muffled giggles then silence, blissful silence. He had got the message, and shoving my head back under the pillow, fell quickly to sleep before he decided on a repeat performance.

Next morning, we met at breakfast. After a few hours' sleep I was feeling a touch more benevolent, but still looked completely wrecked. I could hardly believe my eyes; Robbie looked as fresh as a daisy. I had hardly expected him to put in an appearance at all after all his exertions.

"I'm sorry if you were kept from your beauty sleep last night," he said not looking at me, busy spreading a thick layer of butter and jam onto a slice of toast, reminiscent of a bricklayer. I sighed, still miffed.

Not so much as a trace of remorse, have you, Robbie?

"Last night AND this morning!" I corrected, helping myself to cornflakes. "Look, Robbie, I'm not really interested in your so-called 'achievements'. For all I care you can sleep with the entire female population of the county, but if you could just keep the noise down a bit, I would be grateful and so, I suspect would half the corridor. Can't you shove a sock in their mouths or something?"

He raised his eyebrows suggestively and leered. "Sorry honey! Can't help it if I'm irresistible to beautiful women."

"Clean your glasses, Robbie," I said spluttering on a flake of cereal. "That one last night looked a bit of a dog." He thumped me on the back a bit too hard, dislodging the offending crumb.

"Takes a bitch to know another bitch Paola dear."

"You be careful or you'll catch something nasty one day," I said wagging my spoon. He laughed dismissively.

"You sound just like my Mother. Anyway, life's for living. Live every day as though it were your last, because one day it will be and you never know when that day will come." I hoped he didn't think I looked like his Mother.

"Anyhow," he continued, licking butter and jam from his fingertips with relish, "Are you doing anything particular today?"

"No," I answered, suspicious that he was going to ask me to darn his socks or something. "Why?"

"I thought that you being a country gal and all, that you would like to show me around the place maybe."

I hesitated, trying to think of an excuse.

"Oh, come on Pao! I borrowed a car."

"Can you actually drive?" I asked, a little worried.

"Tractors and Chevies," he said beaming, as I gave him a long hard look across the table.

"Just so long as you haven't got me pencilled in as your next achievement, Robbie," I said.

"I would not dare to presume. It's a deal then. Right, go get your woollies. It's cold outside."

***

"Where on earth did you get this car, Robbie?" I stared at the beautiful machine parked outside the entrance to the Nurses' Home. "Who do you know for Heaven's sake that would trust you with a car like that?"

"Oh, I have a few contacts you know," he said furtively tapping the side of his nose with a finger.

"It's not stolen is it? I am not going out in a stolen car!"

"No, it is not stolen. Now get in, will you?" He opened the door of the turquoise blue Consul Capri 335 and pushed me into the passenger seat. "I have one like this back home; 1961, 1340cc engine, rear fins, twin headlamps, two-speed wipers and a cigar lighter!

"You don't smoke," I said, trying not to sound impressed.

Ignoring me, he waxed lyrical for a further ten minutes on what was 'under the hood' and how exciting it was to drive. He could have been the Ford Motor Company's head salesman; he certainly was its greatest fan.

Grudgingly though I had to admit that it was a very good-looking car and as I idly ran my fingers over the leather interior fittings I began to understand the attraction. Apparently, not many were made and 'she' was a rare model, manufacture only lasting two years.

Robbie proved to be a better driver than I had expected and we soon found ourselves heading on the M1 motorway past Sheffield and towards Leeds. We drove on without stopping until we reached Pickering in North Yorkshire on the edge of the Lake District National Park. Although cold, the sun stayed out and it was pleasant to wander through the old town, with its lovely quaint shops. Then after morning coffee, we drove on to Haworth and visited the Parsonage.

It was something that Robbie had been really keen to do, having read the books by the Bronte sisters in his childhood. He was impressed by the old Parsonage, as all who visit cannot fail to be, but particularly Americans, who seem to love our history.

We wandered its tiny, quaint rooms, where the famous and talented family had been raised. One particular upstairs bedroom looked out over the path to the church where Patrick Bronte, their Father, was clergyman and where the family would have walked together going to and from worship all those years ago.

The gardens on either side, were beautiful, even in winter; a typical English country garden, which in summer would have been resplendent with the colour and scent of delphiniums, lupins, old fashioned climbing roses and lavenders. During my childhood I had been here many times throughout all the seasons and was thoroughly enjoying sharing the memories with Robbie, filling the gaps in his knowledge.

For once, I had the upper hand and could tell him something that he didn't already know, but I really had no need to impress him; the building, with its atmosphere, did that.

Haworth Parsonage had been built in 1778. In the same year Captain James Cook discovered the Hawaiian Islands, naming them the Sandwich Islands, William Pitt, the British Prime Minister died and in America, the Revolutionary War was raging.

In 1820, Patrick Bronte, his wife Maria and their six children moved in, but happiness was to be short-lived. After Maria's untimely death in 1821, Aunt Branwell arrived to care for the family, as the young ladies and their brother, the poet; Branwell Bronte had to be supervised.

Wandering around the house, Robbie and I spoke in hushed voices, conscious of past genius still present within the very fabric of the building, as if fearful of disturbing it. We came upon one of Charlotte's dresses, displayed in a glass case. How tiny she must have been. The waist on the gown must have measured no more than sixteen inches and its matching shoes looked as if they had been made for a child.

We entered what would have been the dining room, where apparently, most of the novels were written. In order to get their first books published, the sisters adopted the pseudonyms of Currer, Ellis and Acton Bell, suggesting that they were male. As women, they would have stood little chance of being published otherwise.

"Just think," I said softly, "Those wonderful stories may never have seen the light of day because of the belief that a woman couldn't possibly produce anything worthy of publication. Thank goodness for that lie, but it was typical of how women were viewed at the time and no-one understood that better than the sisters."

"I wonder what she really looked like," said Robbie, "Charlotte I mean. I must have read 'Jane Eyre' a dozen times; that book fascinated me when I was growing up." He smirked at me, eyebrows raised. "I suppose you think it a strange choice for a boy to read; my Mother's influence I'm afraid. She ensured that we got some culture into our souls, one way or another."

I was impressed. There was more to this brash American than met the eye and I was beginning to like him, rather a lot.

"I always imagined her as a diminutive woman, probably given to the vapours, with hair scraped back and large cow-eyes," said Robbie, "and a pale, delicate skin."

"There's a portrait!" I said, remembering. "Come on I'll show you. It was of all three sisters, painted by brother Branwell. If memory serves, she is the one on the right." I consulted the guide-book. "Yes, that's right."

I lead him to an adjoining room where it hung; a bit creased with age. Robbie stared at it, his face breaking into a smile.

"That is exactly how I imagined her to look," he whispered, eyes locked on Charlotte's. "I can almost feel them here, a part of the history of this place. I wish I could tap into that creativity for just a moment. It's easy to feel their closeness in a place like this; doesn't take much talent at all." He winked at me.

"That's very profound," I said, "For you!"

"Aaah," he sighed, tapping his nose, "there's a lot of things you don't know about me."

"No doubt." I raised my eyebrows. There was something about the way he said it, that made me uncomfortable for a moment or two, before it passed; something that was not quite right.

Americans seem to be rather impressed by both our history and aristocracy. Maybe, because they haven't got much of their own to speak of and we had to stop on the journey back each time we passed a country house of any size, so he could take photos of it. I'm afraid it was the sort of thing I took for granted.

Eventually, his film ran out and we stopped at a lovely little country pub and ordered sandwiches, then played like children on the swings in the park next door for a while, before returning inside to warm ourselves by the log fire and have a couple of beers. It was the first time Robbie had tasted English beer and he was unimpressed.

"This beer is warm!" he retorted. "Ugghhh!"

"Now don't go making a fuss," I scolded. "That's the way we drink it over here." Apparently, all drinks 'back home', came with ice.

"What is it?" he asked in disgust peering into the glass and grimacing. "It's called Newcastle Brown," I explained, afraid he might pour it into the nearest plant pot. "It 'nukes' your tubes on the way down." He made a face then proceeded to drink it after all.

"You should try Bourbon," said Robbie wiping his mouth with the back of his hand. "Same effect, but tastes a whole lot better."

"Tell me about America," I said later, as we sat in the car by the river.

"No need Pao. You'll go there yourself one day."

"Not on your Nellie! I exclaimed. "Not if it's full of reprobates like you." He took a playful swipe at me and I ducked.

"Come on," I said, "It's getting cold; let's go home." Suddenly he reached and took my hand in his.

"Thanks for coming out with me today. It meant a lot."

"I bet you say that to all the girls," I said, but somehow I knew he didn't.

Dusk was falling and there was frost in the evening air, producing a magnificent sunset as far as the eye could see stretching off into the west.

"I love sunsets," said Robbie suddenly. "You should see the ones we have back home. Whenever I need to work something out, or just be alone, I climb up to the ridge behind our ranch house, sit amongst the rocks and just gaze at the sky until darkness falls. By then, I usually have an answer. How I love to watch the sun go down. I really miss those sunsets!"

"Don't you dare start getting homesick on me, I chided, trying to lighten the mood before things got any more serious. "Now take me home, you foolish 'Yank!"

We laughed and he started the engine, but not before I caught a strange look in his eyes; a look I had seen before. It was a fleeting sadness that didn't belong there and I was intrigued. I watched him closely as we drove home through the dark night, without speaking.

Yes, I do like you, Robbie, in spite of myself and all the warnings in the world are not going to make me keep away. I have to know you better and why you are so special. I have to know all those secrets you keep hidden, for I know they are there and whether I get hurt or not, I know I must find out.

Chapter Eight

Skye Leighton had been admitted to Princess Margaret ward during our nights off. She was seven years old and as we learned at report time, had come in for investigations, which were not yet complete. For some time she had had recurrent throat and chest infections and was bruising easily. At present, she was covered in a fine rash that neither itched nor went away.

As soon as we had finished the 'hand-over', I went in to see her and was drawn to this most attractive little girl as soon as I saw her.

Skye had long blonde hair, which cascaded down her back. It was the same length, though not the same colour as Linnie's had been. I wondered if her hair was the reason, I was drawn to her. Beneath the rash, she was pale, very pale, weak and obviously unwell.

"Hello Skye," I said introducing myself, sitting on her bed. "What a pretty girl you are and what a beautiful name you have. Do you know there is an island right up at the top of Scotland called Skye? It's very beautiful there too. Now, do you think you will be able to go to sleep tonight?"

"I've been crying for my mummy," came the tiniest of voices, her eyes fixed on my face, probably wondering if she dared to trust me. The trust of a child is the most precious of gifts and once given, must never be compromised. This was one of the first things I learned about Paediatrics and it has served me well ever since that day.

"Does mummy have any other children to look after," I asked, "Do you have any brothers and sisters?"

"No," said the child, a little louder, "Just me."

"Well, maybe mummy will be able to stay with you tomorrow night," I said stroking her hair. Her lip trembled for a moment and turning away, began to cry into her pillow. Pulling up a comfy chair, I scooped her on to my lap, cradling her little body in my arms, gently rocking to and fro.

"Now don't you cry pet," I whispered, smoothing her hair. "If you will just lie there and be brave for a while, I'll come back just as soon as the other little ones have settled. I promise."

"Promise? She ventured her lip still quivering.

"Promise," I said, tucking her teddy bear in beside her.

"Now listen to me teddy!" I said, wagging my finger at him sternly, "You just stay awake and look after Skye for me until I get back." The bear stared at me with a blank expression, but at least the little girl was smiling at last.

"That's better, Skye blue," I said.

"Pink," she whispered softly, pointing to her pink night-gown.

"Okay then, Skye blue pink," I laughed.

"But with spots on!" joined in Robbie, who had popped his head in at the door and had heard the conversation. This made her giggle and I knew that we had won the first round. That was to make friends, lessen her anxiety and to gain her trust in this, the most frightening of settings for a seven-year-old.

Hospitals must be truly terrifying places for small children, but a bit of extra time and effort can make the whole thing so much easier.

***

Over the next few nights, this little charade became a sort of 'battle cry' between the three of us. Skye would peep through the window of her room, which led onto the corridor, watching for us to come on duty. As soon as she saw us, she would call.

"Nurse Paola, it's me! Skye blue!"

"Pink!" I would call back and Robbie would then join in.

"But with great big spots on!" Or perhaps in reverse order, depending on which of us started it. As silly and trivial as it may sound now, it was one of the things that made her happy each night. As before, I kept my promise and when the rest were settled, went to sit with her until she felt sleepy.

"Nurse Paola, tell me a story please," she pleaded, creeping onto my lap, her arms encircling me.

"I have something better than that," I said. "A special song for a very special little girl." I sang the 'Skye boat' song to her.

"Speed bonny boat like a bird on the wing, over the sea to Skye."

"Carry the lad that's born to be king, over the sea to Skye," a rich baritone voice chimed in. I turned, stopping to listen, eyebrows almost disappearing under my hairline. I waited for Robbie to finish the song, captivated by his wonderful voice and shaking my head in disbelief. I turned to look at the child only to find that she was sleeping peacefully, thumb in her mouth.

We left quietly and closed the door. I looked at him intently. What the hell was he doing wasting a talent like that, chasing women and going to medical school?

"Tell me why you are not using a voice like that to do better things than this?" I asked.

"Are there better things than this?"

"You expect me to believe that you have a God-given talent like that and you intend to waste it? You should be at the Royal College of Music at the very least or whatever the equivalent is in the States. I surely can't be the first person to have told you, that to waste a gift like yours is a crime." He raised his eyebrows.

"Robbie," I said, "you never cease to amaze and exasperate me." I set off quickly to clean the steam kettles, with him following close behind.

"And you," he said pointing at me, "You are the singularly most annoying, opinionated woman I have ever set eyes on AND you know far too much for your own good!"

"What?" I asked, puzzled.

"You love kids," he said, following me into the sluice. It was a statement, not a question.

"Of course," I said, "I've made myself a promise that one day I will have a dozen! That's if I can ever find a suitable man." He was serious now, fixing me with an intense gaze.

"Oh, do excuse me, Ma-am," he said, with more than a hint of sarcasm. "If you reach for the moon, you'll probably only get halfway up the tree, if you are lucky. But there's no harm in dreaming Pao. Dreams stop us from going crazy in this lousy world, where little kids get ill and die."

I opened my mouth to reply, but he cut me off.

"Don't let anyone ever spoil your dream, but you are a terrible hypocrite!" I stared, shocked by his words. "You lecture me about talent and gifts and what I should do. But you see Pao, I know about you! Don't the rules apply to you then? What about the gifts that you ignore every day of your life, except of course when it suits you." He was angry now. "Tell you what lady, you mind your own damn business and I'll mind mine!" With that he turned on his heels and walked away down the corridor, leaving me stunned at his tirade.

***

Skye's Mother and Father had been separated for about a year. When the child became ill, Wendy had tried to find him. All letters to his last known address went unanswered. Jake Barnaby had been a musician, travelling extensively in the past, which had been the main reason for the discord in their relationship. Often he was away for weeks on end, particularly whilst the work was plentiful and the money kept coming in.

The rock scene of mid-sixties was great fun and an exciting place to be if you were single, but for a Mother with a young baby, it was no life. They grew farther apart until Jake left one night, for good, to go and travel with his band, living out of the back of an old camper van. He had written the odd postcard and never forgot Skye's birthday and Christmas, when presents would arrive. But although he sent a little money regularly, in acknowledgement of his continuing responsibility to them both, he remained an absent Father to Skye and a lost love to her Mother.

When Skye had finally been admitted to hospital, Wendy knew she must find him. With a Mother's instinctive fear, she knew that her child was more seriously ill than at first thought, whilst hating herself for even thinking it.

With her child safe in hospital, off she had gone to old haunts, now not quite so comfortable or familiar anymore, determined to find Jake. She knew she must do it, for Skye.

A week later, she found him, after searching for days, around the pubs and clubs of the north of England. With barely any sleep and little time to eat, she had been driven on, until she tracked him down. He had been shocked and concerned, but apparently not enough so, to drop everything and return with her; but although she returned alone, it was with the promise that he would follow in a few days' time.

She now sat by her sleeping child, a Mother's hand on her small head, gently stroking Skye's hair. I gently put my hand on her shoulder so as not to startle her and handed her a cup of tea and a few sandwiches that I'd managed to salvage. She smiled gratefully.

"Thank you so much. I am so relieved to be back with her, my little Skye."

"Wendy, I've found you a mattress," I said. "You can sleep beside her on the floor if you want to. I'll get you some blankets and a pillow. You look all in!"

So, what if it was against all the rules? I didn't care. This child needed her Mother and Wendy needed to be close to her child. I went off to fetch the bedding.

***

The last few years hadn't been kind to Wendy. She'd obviously had a tough time since Jake had left and those times were etched into lines on her face. To support her daughter, she had to go out and get a job for the first time in her life. She had left school without qualifications to follow Jake's dream of 'making it big' in the music business, but it had never really happened.

Before Skye came along, they hadn't needed much, but with the birth of the baby, that had all changed. Babies needed things, food, nappies, and a stable home with a routine. Life on the road was not practical anymore. Row followed row and eventually she moved back closer to her parents, 'just for a little while, until Skye was a bit bigger!'

At first, Jake came home regularly, but as time went by, his visits got less and less and the money he brought to sustain them stopped coming too.

Wendy picked up casual work where she could, in order to support them both, her Mother helping out with Skye. She must have been so tired all the time and had struggled financially for years. It showed.

She was not merely slim, but thin. There is a difference. This was a Mother who fed her child rather than herself, who always clothed Skye, going without warm clothing herself; buying from jumble sales to make what money she had, last to the end of the week. The phrase 'make do and mend' came to mind. She had suffered in a way that Mothers do when there is no alternative, no sacrifice being too great for the love of your child.

In unguarded moments Wendy had a slight look of 'hardness'. It was a barrier she had built around herself, so that nothing could ever get close enough to hurt her again. She was going to need it.

Three nights later, Robbie and I came on duty to the news that Skye's test results were back, confirming that she had Acute Lymphatic Leukaemia and in her case the prognosis was terrible. She had the disease in its worst possible form.

The little girl had a few short weeks to live. Even with aggressive treatment, which was to begin at once, no-one could give her more than a few months.

Standing quietly by her bed during the night, I gazed tearfully at her as she slept. This precious, beautiful child was going to die. Her lovely blonde hair, which I had just plaited for her, would fall out; the toxic effects of the chemotherapy drugs. These medicines, and there wasn't a great deal of choice in those days, were of course, deadly poisons themselves. In destroying the cancer cells, it wasn't always possible to protect normal healthy ones, as the drugs could not discriminate between the two.

Today we can target abnormal cells precisely, leaving healthy ones undamaged, but then, cancer therapy was still in its infancy.

I spent a long time watching Skye that night, each moment bringing with it, sheer helplessness and increasing anger. In spite of all our love and care, drugs, blood transfusions and all the wishing in the world, nothing could be done to change the outcome.

It is so different today. Research has triumphed and given us the tools to fight this awful disease. Better use of selective drugs and bone-marrow transplants have revolutionised the treatment of childhood Leukaemia, to the effect that ninety-five per cent are curable and all are treatable.

But not then: not for poor Skye. We had too few guns in our arsenal for the battle for her life to be won.

Wendy wore the stunned look that you see etched on the faces of earthquake survivors as they sit amongst the rubble, hopeless and helpless, tearstained faces in unimaginable pain. She had wrapped herself in a cloak of grief, which no-one could penetrate, because the only thing she had left in the world was about to be taken away, her beloved little girl. Who could blame her for wanting to shut out the world which had been the source of such cruelty, sitting day after day, night after night, beside her child, comforting, stroking and holding her, never letting her eyes wander away for very long.

All through my nights off, I was unable to get Skye out of my mind, eventually giving in and wandering up to the children's ward to peer through the glass, only to see her lost beneath intravenous drips, surrounded by equipment.

When I returned to duty, her lovely hair had already begun to fall out and her mouth had started to bleed. Carefully I wiped her pale lips and gave her a drink.

"Hello Skye blue," I whispered softly.

"Pink." She was barely able to form the word, but she opened her eyes and I knew she was looking for Robbie. Of course, the last part of our trio was missing.

"He's not here tonight darling," I said gently, "probably wining and dining some lovely lady, but he'll be here tomorrow night, I promise."

She smiled weakly and moved her head to get more comfortable, leaving a loose strand of blonde hair on the soft pillow. Unseen, I plucked it away, swallowing against a hard lump that had formed in my throat.

"You try to go to sleep now my pet," I whispered, tears threatening to brim over my eyelids. "I'll be back very soon, I promise," and running to the sluice-room, scrubbed the steam kettles until they shone!

Sometimes it all became too much to bear. Such was that night, when raw emotions were running high, it was necessary to divert and do other things to keep busy and occupy your mind with happier things.

The rest of the children on the ward weren't particularly ill, mostly recovering from minor operations or injuries. It never ceased to amaze me, how kids with legs in plaster casts were still capable of kicking a football around at high speed, not hesitating from upending anyone who got in the way.

After successfully returning our budding goal-keeper back in his bed, I turned my attention to a scrapping pair of nine-year-old boys, engaged in a fight to the death over the affections of an eight-year-old girl with appendicitis and rampant head lice!

How simple life is when you are nine and my how your priorities change as you grow older.

With peace restored, I treated myself to an illicit cup of tea behind the kitchen door and a nightly 'cuddle round' of the babies.

Sitting there in the dim light of one of the far end balconies, a tiny mite, slumbering in my arms, Linnie suddenly popped into my mind with a rush, reminding me of something she had once said.

Believe in yourself and your abilities, but above all listen!

I realised then, that I hadn't heard her speak to me again since that Christmas Eve. I'd seen her in the meadow the day I was ill, but she hadn't spoken. How easy, when your mind is on other things to forget the advice of a good friend.

I was desperate to hear her voice, to speak to her again, if only for a short time. Maybe I wasn't allowing her to come. Possibly, I wasn't listening hard enough and then only when it suited me. I knew I had to stop being so selective and to start being proud of what I had, as opposed to being a little embarrassed about it. I had always been a little afraid to tell people and I certainly hadn't told Robbie, afraid of becoming a figure of ridicule; 'the crazy woman who hears voices'.

The exception, of course, was Shelagh. Although she often made fun of me, she accepted me the way I was, but then again, the Irish also believe in 'the little people!' Linnie was right! It was high time I started listening again.

I returned the baby to his cot, bent to kiss him and decided there and then to stop feeling sorry for myself. There I was, criticising Robbie for not using his talents, whilst being just as guilty myself and so, standing by the door in the gloom, I closed my eyes and took a deep breath, exhaling slowly the way I had done as a child.

Help me through this, Linnie, for I cannot do this alone. Stay close by my side, as you did when we were together. Send me help, for I have so much to learn. Nothing happened. I took another breath and concentrated hard. A tiny pin-prick of light, broke through the darkness, deep behind my eyes, spreading throughout my conscious mind in a wonderful purple haze and I felt it surround me like a 'comfort blanket and with it came the faintest whiff of Blue Grass'.

She's near! I know she's near!

Whisper followed whisper, rising to a jumble of voices, each trying to be heard. As I breathed in the peace they brought, strength and purpose returned with each inspiration. After a few minutes, I opened my eyes and as they adjusted to the dim light of the ward, I knew that I was once again surrounded by the love of old friends.

I made the momentous decision to tell Robbie all about it the very next night. I didn't care if he laughed, or thought I was crazy. I would no longer hide it. If I was happy with the way I was, it was not important what anyone else thought. I decided to wait until we were on duty and it was quiet, so I could recount the whole thing without interruption. I would wait until we were in a confined space, so he couldn't escape to his room, lock the door and hang garlic about the place.

***

Robbie was unusually quiet on the walk to work, the following night.

"All right then!" I said after a couple of exploratory sideways glances, "What's up?"

"I was stood up last night," he said with incredulity, as though no-one in their right mind would even contemplate doing such a thing.

"Good for her, whoever she was!" I exclaimed, a little unkindly. "I knew someone would wise up to your antics eventually." He looked genuinely hurt.

"Not only that, but she phoned me up and gave me a real verbal slammin'. Called me a rat. You don't think I could be losing it, do you, Pao?"

"Oh, definitely!" I replied, relishing his discomfort, "Either that or all your so-called 'achievements' have got their heads together at long last to get their revenge. If I were you, I'd look out for women carrying sharp implements." I was finding it increasingly difficult to keep a straight face.

"There was a young fella' called Reg," I recited, "who took a girl down by a hedge, along came his wife with a big carving knife and cut off his meat and two veg. Boom Boom!" I finished and burst out laughing.

"Bitch!" he yelled, taking a swipe at me and missing before joining in the joke.

***

Skye was very ill.

"Her mum's with her," said Sister Thomas kindly, at report time. Do what you can for them both."

I looked down at the still, pale child in the bed, and knew she was dying.

Lowering the cot-side I lifted her carefully onto my lap. She murmured and tried to open her eyes, but was too weak for even that small task. Her eyelids fluttered and a tiny muscle on her cheek twitched. What remained of her pigtail was draped pathetically over her shoulder. She gurgled like a baby, content after its feed, fluid collecting in her throat.

Suddenly, as with some supreme effort, her eyes opened wide and looked directly into mine. With gathering terror, I held her gaze.

"Mummy!" said a small voice, "Get mummy quick." Skye's lips had not moved.

***

"Wendy!" I cried, "Wendy! Where are you?" She wasn't there. She must have gone out for some fresh air or a drink! "Robbie, Robbie!" I called insistently, the tone of my voice bringing him running. He stared at the sight, stopped in his tracks.

"It's Skye! She's…" I began, unable to say the word.

"I know. I'll get Wendy," he called over his shoulder as he hurried away.

As I rocked her gently in my arms, being careful to give her comfort, not pain, her eyes flickered, half-open, trying to focus. She was making strange sounds as she breathed and I instinctively reached for the oxygen mask, knowing that it would make no difference.

Please not yet! I prayed. Not just yet. This child needs her Mother. Hang on, little one. Please don't take her yet. Just a few moments longer, please!

Just as my head felt as if it were about to burst, there came the sound of running footsteps, heavy through the otherwise still night.

"Thank you, thank you," I cried aloud looking Heavenward. "He found her, he found Wendy. Thank you!" They both stopped, stock still in the doorway, horrified, then Wendy walked toward me slowly, suddenly calm and in control, with a dignity, I wished I had possessed at that moment.

"Is it time?" she asked simply.

"I think it is," I answered tearfully, meeting her steady gaze.

"Hand her to mummy now." A gentle, but firm voice said from behind me.

"Wendy," I whispered, my voice cracking, "take her from me."

She held out her arms and took the child, holding her close as only a Mother can do, caressing the child's brow with her lips. Skye briefly opened her eyes and reached out to touch her Mother's face in a final physical contact.

Weeping unashamedly now, I watched as the lights came, blues and purples swirling all around them, swaddling Mother and child softly, as they locked together in a final embrace. I watched as the room was bathed in a soft, translucent glow, far too beautiful for anything of this world.

No more pain now, no more suffering.

Then she was gone from the shell which lay in her Mother's arms, as tender hands carried her upwards and onwards, far from the troubles of this world, pillowing her away on the softest gossamer breeze, to a place of pure crystal light.

***

We stood in the sluice room, Robbie and I, side by side, silently looking out into the night.

"Sod it!" I exclaimed suddenly, giving way to tears again, and we put our arms around each other, holding on tightly for the mutual comfort it brought after such a heart-rending tragedy.

"Sometimes I wonder what I'm doing here," said Robbie, at last breaking away and wiping his face on the sleeve of his tunic, already streaked black with my mascara.

"What are you doing here Robbie?" I asked, between sniffs. He wet a towel, passing it to me to wipe the smudges from my face, and sighed deeply.

"Oh, just trying to reconcile a few things in one part of my life, so that I can get on with the rest of it. So far, Pao, it's not proving as easy as I expected."

"What things?" I said not wanting to give up so easily this time.

"I'll tell you all about it soon Pao," he answered with a sincerity I had never heard from him before. "I promise, but not tonight, not now. Tonight had taken a huge chunk out of me. You see, I never saw a child die before and I hope I never have to see another."

"Nor me," I whispered sadly, "but I know that perhaps I shall. Do you think it will ever get any easier? It hurts so much at the moment and I can't imagine why I would want to put myself through this again. How do you move on from something so horrible as we've witnessed tonight and be expected to carry on as normal?"

The door opened slowly and a small freckled face peered round.

"Nurse Paola, I wet the bed!" Robbie and I looked at each other and laughed gently.

"I think that was your answer," said Robbie picking up the small, damp, ginger-haired boy. "Let's get you changed and into a dry bed, soldier!"

"Can you reconcile your problems?" I asked as we walked back to the main ward.

"I don't have a choice," said Robbie, "There are some things you just can't run away from.

"You are a strange man to understand Robbie and quite the most exasperating one I ever met in my life, but we all have our secrets and there are things I have to tell you too."

"Okay!" he nodded. "After this set of nights then. I guess we both owe each other an explanation."

"Nothing's owed," I said.

"Okay then!" he repeated, "if for no other reason, then for friendship," and with that he kissed me on the forehead.

I paused outside the window of Skye's room for a moment, the curtains drawn across the window.

"Goodbye, Skye," I whispered, "and may God bless you, wherever you are."

However, that wasn't quite the end of the story.

***

Despite the Vet's dire warning, I did, in fact, go on to become a Midwife after completing my general Nurse Training. It was one of the best decisions of my life, for I found my niche at last and the start of a life-long love affair with delivering babies. The joy it has given me over the years is immeasurable, despite its many trials and tribulations. Only managing to have one baby of my own, after ten years of trying, all the indignities that go along with the fertility clinic stay in the memory for a long time.

I am eternally grateful, therefore, to all those Mothers who selflessly allowed me to indulge myself and share their joy, even for a short time. One of the greatest privileges is to be there when new life comes into this world and even more so when you can play a small part in the process.

Even after thirty-five years I still get a tremendous buzz each time I deliver a baby and adore being surrounded by them on a daily basis.

One night, whilst working as a hospital-based Midwife, I admitted a lady in the late stages of labour and she seemed vaguely familiar, but during ten years of regular night duty, I saw an awful lot of Mothers and their babies, sometimes several times over! It was a really busy Maternity Unit and most nights, something of a production line, being one of only two units left in the country that had ante-natal, delivery suite, post-natal and nursery all together on each ward.

Between her contractions, we chatted and I wondered initially if I had delivered her before, but her first child had been born long before I had done my training. Sometimes people in that situation just seem familiar.

In the early hours, my colleague delivered her of a lovely son, as I had already had three deliveries that night. I went in for 'the catch', as we call it; that is the second Midwife who is responsible for attending to any immediate needs of the newborn, such as drying him, clearing his airway if required and handing him to his Mother. This leaves the delivering Midwife free to exclusively attend to the woman.

All went well, baby being born quickly, after a short labour and with the minimum of effort. Women don't generally 'hang about' by the time it gets to the second baby; having done it before a woman's body generally knows what it's doing with little interference from the 'experts'.

When it was over, I took in a tray of tea and biscuits and withdrew, leaving the new little family to get to know each other in private, before the baby was removed to the nursery at the end of the ward, which was the custom in those days.

A couple of hours later, I sat in the nursery feeding that particular infant, whilst his Mother slept. He had been howling a moment ago, leaving no-one in any doubt that his tummy needed filling. Now, plugged into his bottle he fed contentedly, nose wrinkling with each suck.

"What a splendid fellow you are," I told him, lowering my voice in that unique way women do when they talk to small babies. As he continued to wolf down his milk, I rocked him gently, humming a tune.

Suddenly, like a thunderbolt, a thought hit me.

Good grief! I was certain I knew his Mother. No, it couldn't be. Surely not!

I looked down into the face of the now content baby and realised what I had been humming. It was the 'Skye Boat Song!'

Returning the sleeping infant to his crib, I hurried down the ward to the Office and closed the door behind me, searching the desk for the Mother's medical notes. Light-headed and shaking, all my fingers seemed to be thumbs, as I fumbled to turn the pages, scanning the words before me, excitement building.

Josephine Wendy Marshall… address… date of birth… I read on, with face flushed and heart racing. Previous obstetric history… 1962… normal delivery of live female infant… six pounds two ounces… Breastfed… Present pregnancy… First child of second marriage… NB: CHILD DIED AGED SEVEN YEARS… LEUKAEMIA

Shocked, I dropped the notes and pressed both hands over my mouth, then rechecked the maiden name again, twice, just to be sure. "Skye!" I said aloud. There was no mistake and standing in the office for what seemed like an eternity, the memories flooding back and with them, long-buried emotions. I fought for control.

"Bloody 'ell! Ger 'old o'thissen an' don't be such a prat!" shouted an all too familiar voice behind my left ear. I'd had quite a few different guides down the years, but no-one who came close to this larger-than-life character who I called 'Alf'. He certainly did not mince his words. "Tha' should know be now, that where theeze loss, thill allus be gain. Nah fer God's sake woman, give ovver roarin' an' get that bloody kettle on!"

***

"Hello, Wendy," I said. It was morning.

"Oh, I'm so glad you recognised me, "she said, her eyes lighting up her still lovely face. "I really didn't know whether to say anything or not."

"I am so glad you did!" I said, hugging her. "I wasn't sure you would want to remember something so painful. Losing your child is just about the worst thing that can happen to a person. Not everyone would want to remember anyone associated with that memory."

Wendy patted the bed, motioning me to sit beside her and when I had, she began to talk.

***

"When Skye died, a huge part of me died too; if fact for a very long time afterwards, I wished that I had. I had nothing in the world left to live for you see. Her Father never did come, did he?" She gave a resigned smile. "How fragile are those promises we all hang on to. I often wondered whether perhaps things would have been different if he had come back. It took two long years before I could even think of myself as having any sort of future. Then there was the divorce, another compounding blow just to make sure I didn't get up again after the disabling grief of losing Skye. My life was nothing and I decided to finish it with an overdose and planned it for the following day. I was so together about it and so relieved that at last there would be closure and I had the best night's sleep I'd had for years.

I woke next day to the sun streaming through the window and knew exactly what I had to do and so, packing what few bits I had, bought an air ticket and went off on the adventure of a lifetime. To this day, I still don't know where I got the courage."

"I know," I whispered softly.

"Yes Paola, I think perhaps you do!" Her eyes looked deep into mine. "Skye was the loveliest and happiest little girl in the world and maybe that was her way of telling me that life goes on. If I'd done something stupid, then her life and all those precious years we had together would have counted for nothing.

I travelled round Europe and on to the Middle East and then to Singapore, picking up work as I went and hitching when the money got low. I never gave it a second thought; just 'packed my traps' and went. If I had stopped to think too hard, then I wouldn't have done it and that would have been a shame, because it was by far the best decision I ever made. It put my life back in perspective and at last, I was able to put the past where it belongs; in the past.

On the way back through Italy, I met Simon, who was doing something similar, though not for the same reasons, thank goodness, and as you can see," she said, smiling adoringly at the newborn infant, "the rest is history."

"And are you content Wendy?" I asked. "Have you found happiness again?"

"Truly," she said her eyes glowing with happiness. "I loved Skye with all my being and I always will, but I've moved on to a new life now, with a new kind of love. It's not based on regret, or longing for what might have been; we can't change the past. My life is based on what's here and now and it's wonderful. Do you think that sounds really selfish Paola?"

"I think," I said, picking up the stirring baby, "That it sounds just about right to me!" He opened one eye and wrinkled his brow. "Do you know," I asked him seriously, "what a very lucky boy you are?"

"Fer Chrissakes woman! Gi' that babby back to 'is mam and stop pissin' abaht," interjected my uncouth friend loudly.

I said my 'good-byes' to Wendy and her child; this time in much happier circumstances and walked briskly back up the ward, grinning broadly.

She had her happy ending at last and so did I!

Chapter Nine

We reached the final morning of our stint of night duty at last and as we walked sleepily back to the Nurses' Home our beds beckoning, I persuaded Robbie to audition for the hospital's annual show.

Playing on his vanity, I told him that his singing talent was far too good to waste and anyway, we didn't have too many singers with natural ability. Plenty of us could make a passable noise and more or less hold a tune. After all, nobody really minded a few questionable notes. It was all tremendous fun, with everyone joining in. To my astonishment, he agreed straight away. Maybe we all needed a bit of light relief after recent events.

I had been involved in drama most of my life and loved it. As small children we had been drafted into the annual village show; written, devised, produced and directed by one of the teachers from the primary school where Annie and I went.

It was a 'black and white minstrel show;" not 'politically correct' now of course, but in the sixties, life was far more simple.

There were no black people living in our little village and very few in the local town. The only black person we ever saw was old Mrs Parminter-Jackson, who made the costumes. She lived in a little cottage high above the village.

Mrs Eleanor Parminter-Jackson, had come to England after the war with her English husband, Frederick, so we didn't really count her as very different. Some of the sillier children said she was a witch, as she made and sold birch brooms, locally called 'besoms'. I can't imagine she made much money, as they were very sturdy and lasted for years. We probably still have one in the shed!

Mrs Jackson didn't seem in the least offended by the men 'blacking up' and singing 'Negro-spiritual' songs which were, after all remnants from slave trade and undoubtedly would have affected her ancestors coming from that part of the world.

Folk regarded her as a bit of a curiosity at first, but after a while, no-one even seemed to notice that she was black and she certainly was black.

During rehearsals, she would knit constantly; a large ball of wool on her capacious lap, needles clicking at a frantic rate, often in perfect time to the music. If any of the smaller children got weary or fractious during rehearsals, she would scoop them up into her lap, tousled heads resting against her equally large bosom. They would sleep contentedly as she stroked their hair; knitting abandoned for the time being, in favour of a more important task; her lap well-loved by the majority of us children.

But it was her clothes, with their exotic colours and smells, which fascinated us as kids, with their voluminous folds of brightly coloured material, encircling her large body; it was possible to spot her coming from quite a distance. This was the early fifties and the austerity of those post-war years remained, at least in our area of the country. Brightly coloured fabrics were not to appear in the shops for a few years yet! Mrs EPJ (as she was known to all,) must have seemed a rare and colourful bird indeed!

It is with real affection that I remember those theatrical events with all their larger-than-life characters, for not only were we allowed to show off unashamedly, but they were very ordered, well-planned affairs which taught us discipline, whilst having the time of our lives.

***

The hospital show was, in complete contrast, chaotic in the extreme, with everyone wanting to do something. Fortunately, not everyone wanted to act; many opting for the equally important, though less glamorous roles of set-building, scenery painting or the most vital job of all, making the tea!

There was never any shortage of actors either and we had to hold auditions for the best parts, often with great rivalry between the various wards and departments. It just went to show how many exhibitionists there were around. The show provided a wonderful opportunity to lose our inhibitions for a short time and generally show off! Much more important, was that we were allowed to poke fun at the authoritarian figures around the hospital and for once, get away with it. Singled out for particular 'attention', were the consultants and the nursing hierarchy. Because it was a special occasion, they came in for a lot of 'stick', taking it with reasonably good humour.

A few of us joined forces to write scripts and sketches, as early as September and by now the work was in full swing, creativity oozing out of every pore. We would gather at night in someone's room, to write and bounce ideas around, usually surrounded by empty beer cans and disgustingly overflowing ashtrays.

These drunken gatherings often went on into the wee small hours, as we couldn't' get started until Tissie had done her 'bed round'. Anyway, humour came much more readily with a few beers inside you, oiling the muscles and those brain cells responsible for creativity.

As far as writing and performing were concerned, the junior doctors were always a good source of talent. In short, they were generally willing to do almost anything for the promise of a few beers and a late-night grope. Whilst at medical school, many of them had got involved in stunts for university 'rag days' and were no strangers to making fools of themselves! 'Residency', or the doctors' living quarters, were of course, strictly 'out of bounds' to nurses. There was, however, more than one way in!

The long-established myth, that every nurse's dream is to marry a doctor needs some clarification.

Most doctors are of the opinion that nurses belong to a different species and vice-versa. Almost all regard us as their subordinates. We nurses, on the other hand, have strong ideas to the contrary. Away from the wards, both groups tend to move in completely different circles, providing an excellent basis for conflict and not romance; passion, maybe, but as every woman over thirty will swear, the two are completely unconnected.

The scenario, which forms the basis of many a romantic novel, has doctor and nurse, falling in love over the operating table or eyes meeting across a sick patient and truly belongs in the realms of fiction. Reality is just not like that.

The average Theatre Nurse would be much more likely to report that she spent her time dodging instruments, when 'Sir' lost his temper and all was not going well. I myself worked in theatre with an exceedingly grumpy consultant who, on occasions, threw the scalpel, complaining that it wasn't sharp. It was however as I vividly recall, damn sharp enough to stick in the wall alongside my head, quivering like a dagger.

As for gazing into each other's eyes in the depths of night whilst mopping fevered brows, well… The nurses might just have been wide-awake in the early hours, but when a doctor had been begrudgingly ousted from his bed, for what was, in his opinion not a very good reason, dialogue was generally unwise.

Sensible nurses disappeared to the sluice room until the grumpy old so-and-so had been and gone, rendering romance out of the question.

The principal that relationships will flourish, when two people work closely together is sound enough. It may happen, particularly in the presence of high emotion, but I have found that this is the exception rather than the rule.

The catalyst is the male/female attraction and not who wears the white coat. After a few months, not many nurses are still impressed by a white coat, particularly when its occupant turns up smelly, bad-tempered and unkempt in the middle of the night. Medicine is really not a job for anyone who wants to impress the women!

Now with the daylight, the white coat's occupant changes to someone who is well turned out, good-looking and saves lives and there are few things more attractive than that.

We, as nurses, are our own worst enemy, forever burdened by a small minority, hell-bent on marrying a doctor at all costs. The rest of us will settle for love and don't care a toss whether or not he has letters after his name. Over the years there have been many alternative suggestions, as to what 'FRCS (Fellow of the Royal College of Surgeons) should really stand for!

The one thing on which nurses all agree is that we would gladly settle for the recognition as fellow professionals in our own right. Forget the handmaiden, gazing up into the face of a white-coated Adonis, hanging on his every word and then clearing up the mess after him. Television had an awful lot to answer for!

This image was why a certain horrible little resident called Jonathan Lockley was so despised.

He made a habit of strutting around in a self-important way, unendearing to everyone. Even at mealtimes, his stethoscope remained around his neck. It was as though it made him feel important; he probably wore it on his day off too, as no-one would have given him a second glance otherwise.

Jonathan was twenty-eight, his hair already thinning on top and he had those 'podgy' greasy features you see in teenage boys prone to acne. His most outstanding feature, literally, was his large flat-ended nose, which seemed to have a permanent drip. With no eyebrows and little facial hair, he had the unfortunate appearance of a snuffling pig. Poor Jonathan! Not the best looking of men.

In spite of what his dressing mirror must have told him on a daily basis, he was in love with himself and expected everyone else to feel the same. He was not tall, standing around five foot eight at the most, but in the eyes of Jonathan Loxley; a physical, mental and intellectual giant of a man.

However, despite his enormous ego, he was a social misfit, with no other conversation save for medicine and so, was never invited to any of the parties.

These booze-ridden, illicit social events, held in the doctors' quarters, were usually organised by the nurses, so it was not surprising that Jonathan developed a deep-seated hatred of all of us.

He never made any secret of the fact that he despised all nurses and treated us appallingly. He said we were 'spoilt, stand-offish bitches, only good for one thing!'

He obviously felt that the sole purpose of a nurse was to do his bidding and we all had our own ideas about that!

In the past, he had made somewhat creepy advances to one or two of the new nurses, but on each occasion had been thwarted. I don't think he ever had a proper girlfriend in his life and some would say 'No wonder!'

Jonathan's one success in life had been to qualify from Medical school. There was no question that he was good at his job, but his skill with inter-personal relationships was non-existent. He really had no idea how to speak to people on a social level, or any other level for that matter. He firmly believed that he should command instant respect because he was a doctor and that everyone else should understand that. He was of the opinion that he alone stood aloft from everyone else further down the food chain.

Jonathan was a 'house-resident', meaning that he was a newly qualified doctor in his first year of proper practice; a very steep learning curve, even if you were lucky enough to have everyone from the consultant to the ward cleaner on your side. Jonathan however, believed he was above all that, firmly of the opinion that as he was the best thing ever to grace the wards; he needed no help from anyone.

We all waited with bated breath for the day when Jonathan Lockley would fall flat on his podgy little face; no-one dreaming that when it happened, that there would be so many delighted onlookers present to join in the fun and the retribution.

So thoroughly fed up with being ignored, left out of things generally and not getting the girl, Jonathan Lockley decided that he would get his own back on everyone. He made up his mind to be the star of the Christmas show, finally proving to the world what a wonderful and thoroughly decent fellow he was.

Now Jonathan knew that he was not at the top of anyone's Christmas card list and that in order to 'get in' he would have to make sacrifices. He would have to be nice to people… people he wasn't used to being nice to: The Nurses!

That was his main problem, these being the same nurses whom he would verbally abuse, whenever they had the misfortune to work with him and nurses have very long memories.

He was a swine to work with. Whenever he performed any procedure he took delight in scattering both dirty dressings and other paraphernalia far and wide, deliberately dropping needles and instruments on the floor.

"Go on then girl," he would sneer disparagingly, "don't stand there like a stuffed dummy. Get it all picked up. That's what you're there for!" Whatever the poor patients thought, I do not know, but I'm sure they shared our embarrassment. Patients rarely say anything critical to a doctor, as they feel they hold the power of life and death over them; behaviour I have seen over again in the doctor's surgery.

If the doctors are running late, as they frequently are, patients tend to huddle into groups and complain to each other first, before challenging the poor receptionist and becoming thoroughly offensive.

"How long's he going to be then? I've been sat here ages. Got better things to do, I have you know. I'm going to give 'im a piece o' my mind when I get in there." So it goes on, to and from the desk every few minutes, as they get angrier (and louder) with each patient that goes in, convinced that it was definitely their turn next, whilst grumbling about what they are going to say when they do get in.

Of course, they never do! Something magical happens, between the moment their name is called and the doctor wishing them 'Good morning' and hoping they hadn't been waiting too long.

"Oh, no doctor!" they gush, "It's quite all right. I'm not in a hurry!"

I remain convinced to this day that they think, that if they were to upset him, the doctor may just give them bad news. In this case, 'fear rules'.

Today, of course, the 'Jonathan Lockleys' of this world would not be tolerated. We all respect each other's skills and things are conducted in a far more informal manner, so much better for everyone.

But not then! You did as you were told and some of the job did involve being a 'hand-maiden' to the chap in the white coat, much to my disgust. Jonathan never called any of us by our names, not even 'Nurse'. Mostly, it was, "Hey, you there!" or, "Girl!" I can honestly say that Jonathan Lockley wasn't the most popular person I knew. At the auditions, therefore, a few eyebrows were raised at the latest addition to our happy company, but after all, it was nearly Christmas!

Never was more chaos reeked by a single person! In the first few nights of rehearsal, he managed to knock paint everywhere and all but demolish the set, whilst 'helping' with the carpentry. The following night he managed to spill coffee over the scripts rendering them almost illegible. Shelagh, my friend and our producer was, by now ready to kill him. In an effort to keep him out of everyone's way, some bright spark gave him a saw to hold and he managed to cut his hand so badly as to require a visit to Casualty. Not to be stitched, a large plaster could have taken care of it but he fainted at the sight of his own blood and fell on the set, destroying it a second time.

Tempers were becoming frayed; the very mention of the name 'Lockley', causing Shelagh to scream loudly. It was blatantly obvious to all present, that Jonathan was a walking disaster area!

"Is there anything you can actually do, Jonathan?" I asked diplomatically, a few days later. We were all well aware that he couldn't sing a note. His memorable attempts had sent even the hospital cat running for cover! In spite of everything, I felt a little sorry for him in his desperation to be included.

"Why don't you tell me what you can do, Jonathan," I said, with gentleness undeserved, taking him to one side, "and we'll see if we can work something out." I could see that he was on the edge of desperation.

"I can dance a bit," he said, hand across his mouth so the others couldn't really hear, even if they had been listening.

"You can?" I raised my voice, surprised, "What kind of dancing?" Everyone stopped what they were doing and stared at us, suddenly attentive.

"Ballet!" he mouthed the word at me, silently. My eyes widened, saucer-like as I struggled to keep a straight face, aware that my lip was quivering.

Oh, God, I thought. This is far too good to miss! I suddenly remembered all the comments and all those lousy 'fetch me, carry me, I'm the doctor!' jobs that he had made me do.

"What was that again Lockley? I asked loudly, "Didn't quite hear!"

"Ballet," he retorted defiantly. "If you must know, my Mother used to send me to strengthen my legs." He probably thought that an explanation wouldn't make it seem so bad. I peered down at his legs, trying not to laugh. They looked strong enough to me; perhaps those lessons had worked!

The imagined vision of Jonathan Lockley in tights proved too much for some people, fleeing to the safety of the toilets, howling with uncontrolled laughter as they went. I was determined to keep my dignity at all costs and allow Jonathan to keep his, trying to imagine what it must have taken for the poor fellow to admit to something like that. He really was keen to be in the show, wasn't he? There was a small part of me that admired him, but a much greater part that wanted to see him cringe some more.

I fixed him with a stare, fighting to control the laughter, which threatened to erupt at any moment.

Oh, please don't let me laugh, not now!

"Well then, Jonathan, you had better come along with Shelagh and myself," I said, motioning him to follow, "we'll put on some music and you can show us both your 'entrechat', so to speak."

He followed us quickly, and we went to an adjoining room, away from prying eyes. He looked a bit worried, probably wondering if he had made a big mistake.

Oh, was I going to enjoy this!

To the combined amazement of Shelagh and myself, he was in fact, quite a good dancer. Inventive, when it came to interpreting the music and surprisingly light on his feet; no Gene Kelly, but passable, very passable, which of course, presented us with a dilemma. Had he been absolutely hopeless, we would have had no problem sending him on his way, saying, "Sorry Lockley, stick to medicine, the world isn't ready for you yet!" But now, we had to use him. A quick glance around the rest of the men told us that Lockley was the best prospect so far and we badly needed a male lead for our theme.

"Oh, Shelagh!" I exclaimed as he left the room. "I've a terrible feeling we're going to regret this."

Shelagh and I were in charge of the choreography for this part of the show. We were the only ones with any formal dance training, my Irish friend more so than I was. She had at one time run a small dance school of her own back home.

The theme we had chosen for our part of the show, was the First World War. It comprised three comedy sketches and several dance numbers; then Robbie and I were to close the first half with a duet. The costumes had been borrowed from the local drama group and everything else had been made or stolen.

The first dance number served to set the story of a young man preparing to board a train for France. He was saying a fond 'Goodbye' to his sweetheart, played by Shelagh.

Jonathan knew he was the obvious choice for the soldier and had a permanent smile on his face, realising that 'leaving' usually meant kissing and anticipated that his luck was about to change. Shelagh resigned herself to a fate worse than death, that of having to kiss Lockley, reluctantly agreeing to the supreme sacrifice, for the sake of art!

I had set the moves for the dance and I knew exactly how I wanted it to look, right down to the steam train; to be created, courtesy of Sid the porter and some cylinders of 'dry ice', which had been made to 'disappear' from the Dermatology department. In normal circumstances, 'dry ice' was used to freeze warts off various parts of the body, so the wart-ridden public would just have to wait for a couple of weeks until we took them back.

We reluctantly agreed that Lockley was our man. So far he had behaved impeccably and I began to wonder if this could be the same Lockley we all knew and loved! This harmony, however, was not to last. He reverted to type, just as quickly to become his normal thoroughly unpleasant self, from the moment he knew he was in.

***

The unpleasantness began with the costumes. The local drama group hadn't got a suitably authentic World War One costume to fit Jonathan, so we resigned ourselves to making one. I was fairly handy with a needle and cotton and I knew I could go home on my day off and use Auntie Ivy's old, but much prized and polished, Singer sewing machine. It was worked by a 'treadle'.

You placed your feet flat on a footplate and rocked them forward and back to raise and lower the needle bed, thus sewing. It was great fun. Old Auntie Ivy had proudly taught all us children to sew on it. Apart from the obvious skill of making our own clothes, it quickly taught co-ordination. If your feet didn't move in perfect harmony with your hands when feeding the fabric through, then the needle ran over your fingers. It was a really good incentive to concentrate. When you had picked out the cotton, embedded in your finger a couple of times, believe me, your sewing skills quickly improved!

"Let's get him measured up then," said Shelagh, one evening before rehearsal started. "Come on then Jonathan, get your shirt off!" He was in the habit of wearing a bow tie and those pretentious patterned waistcoats beloved by minor aristocracy. All the other doctors were content with jeans and a T-shirt under their white coats, but not Jonathan; he just had to stand out from the crowd.

Now Shelagh and I had him at a definite disadvantage, half-undressed and vulnerable and he knew it.

"Oh, and the trousers," said Shelagh, smiling happily at him. He looked horrified as we both folded our arms, enjoying his discomfort.

"Is this really necessary?" he asked hesitating, before reluctantly unbuttoning his shirt.

"Don't be stupid Lockley. Can't possibly measure you with your clothes on!" Shelagh retorted, "Anyhow there's only we three here and I doubt you have got anything that would shock the two of us… Have you?" She draped the tape measure around her neck and advanced toward Jonathan menacingly.

"Now look girls," he began, backing away, "I know we have had our differences in the past…" He took off his shirt revealing a string vest. We stared.

"I just knew he would wear a string vest!" I said under my breath as Jonathan quickly unzipped his trousers.

"But that is all in the past, I think we can put all those petty little misunderstandings behind us now. Come on! What do you say?"

"Oh, I bet you do!" we said in unison.

Shelagh's hands tightened menacingly around the tape measure, as advancing, she thrust it around his chest, careful to make as little body contact as possible.

Jonathan leered and winked at her. This was clearly the nearest he had been to a woman in a long time. Shelagh instinctively leaned back, avoiding his breath.

"I think you will find that my chest measurement is forty-two," he told her pompously, still leering and pushing out his rather under-developed pectorals proudly.

"Rubbish!" Shelagh retorted, "Barely measures thirty-six and that's with you shoving it out!"

Without warning, she gave him a sharp stab in the solar plexus with her finger. He coughed, the chest deflating somewhat.

"No need to cough, it's not a medical!" she told him sweetly.

Shelagh had good cause to dislike Jonathan Lockley. One night, on the ward she had overheard him refer to her as 'That thick Irish Witch from the Bogside'. The Irish are immensely proud of the part of Ireland they hail from and to suggest that a Sligo woman from the stunning west coast, came from anywhere else was much more insulting than either of the other two jibes. She had 'marked his card' there and then and had neither forgiven nor forgotten.

So it was with some relish and merely the ghost of an evil smile that she said, "Come on now Jonathan, don't be shy, trousers off! It's alright, no-one is going to come in and see your dangly bits, I promise! That was the idea of coming early, before the others got here." Reluctantly he removed his trousers. The underpants matched the vest.

I glanced at Shelagh and giggled, our thoughts as one.

Well, little chance of him getting a woman if he goes on wearing those!

By now, neither of us dare look at the other, our two pairs of eyes firmly fixed on the mass of knotted string.

Jonathan looked increasingly worried, standing there in his socks, as quickly Shelagh thrust the tape around his waist, read off the measurement and waited for him to argue. He didn't.

"Okay," she said suddenly, dropping to her knees in front of him, "Inside leg!" Giving a small scream, Jonathan jumped back clutching his nether regions in both hands, striking a defiant pose of sheer panic as Shelagh fell back onto her heels, startled.

"For God's sake Lockley!" she yelled, "How the hell am I supposed to measure you with your knees pressed together like a nun on a date? You are always bragging about being a man of the world, so you are. Now, get yer two legs apart so I can do it properly!"

At this point, half a dozen pairs of eyes appeared at the window, attracted by the noise. Thankfully Jonathan had his back to it. Out of his line of sight, I motioned them to disappear. Shelagh threw a pair of trousers at him, her temper wearing thin.

"Here," she said, "Try these on and remember, they are for dancing in, so they are, so they have to be loose and longer to allow you to move."

He put on the trousers, instinctively turning his back on us.

"Now, stand still while I pin them up; move and I'll stick the pins in yer, so I will!" Deftly, she measured the hem and began to pin. "Needs three inches taking off," she said as Jonathan started to wriggle.

"Make them shorter than that woman, or I'll trip up over the bloody things and break my neck. Are you sure you know what you are doing?" Shelagh jabbed in another pin viciously and he yelped.

She looked up at him angrily, her eyes narrowing as she spat the words, "Lockley, you objectionable little man, I know what I am doing. I am measuring them to the floor to allow for your shoes, will you leave this to me?"

Dangerously controlled, she continued to pin.

"You are deliberately trying to make me look stupid, you cow," he spat. "Now take six inches off or at least measure them again, with shoes."

I closed my eyes, trying to imagine how Lockley could possibly look any more stupid than he did at present. "Don't you worry now Jonathan," I said, "This isn't Swan Lake and no-one's going to turn you into a little cygnet."

He replied by turning his full venom on Shelagh and stood looming over her.

"Measure it again, you silly bitch!" he shrieked, his face scarlet with rage.

At that moment I thought that Shelagh was going to hit him, but instead, she carefully took her tape measure and knelt on the ground in front of him and brandishing a large pin, held it, point first against his crotch. For a few tense moments I thought she was going to circumcise him with it, but instead, gave him a wry smile and said firmly, "Oh, I'll measure you all right, but this time Lockley, open your legs and bloody well hold still, will yer?"

Ten people crept silently into the room, just in time to see Shelagh kneeling in front of the half-clad Jonathan both of them absorbed in an activity, not at first glance, obvious. Suddenly and with triumph, Shelagh flung the tape-measure over her head and screamed loudly. "Three inches Lockley! I told you it was no more than three inches!"

***

It took a very long time for poor Jonathan to live down the ribald comments that followed. He became convinced that it was the only thing in his life that he would ever be remembered for and made a pact with himself that one day he would pay the 'Irish

Witch' back, tenfold. At that moment in time, he had no idea how he would do it, only that one day, he would.

We all underestimated him; not one of us guessing the depths to which he would stoop in order to win back his self-respect and get revenge. For Jonathan Lockley, it was to be the most ill-judged and painful decision of his life and one that would nearly end in disaster.

***

The show seemed to occupy my thoughts, most of the time I wasn't working. We were now into the last few weeks of rehearsals and it was time to put all the individual practice together. This was where the whole thing took shape and became a production at last, with all the dance numbers coming together. We had reached the point where everyone had started to work as a team.

Jonathan had been surprised and delighted to discover that Shelagh was to partner him for all his dance numbers, possibly thinking he would be handed an opportunity for retribution sooner than he thought.

Our, otherwise fun-filled and happy company had been infiltrated by such a sullen person; the 'new improved' Jonathan hadn't lasted very long at all. He became more unpleasant than ever, but we refused to let it spoil our fun. He really was his own worst enemy, because no-one spoke to him unless they really had to and he was excluded even more than before. It had been such a brief respite for us all.

I was suspicious and wondered just what he was plotting, surely he wouldn't try to wreck the show out of spite. Anyway, there was far too much to be done to be worrying about such a 'worm' as Jonathan Lockley and we threw ourselves into rehearsals whenever there was a spare moment.

The first dance, though not complicated technically, was very visual and built nicely to a climax. Shelagh, as 'the sweetheart', was required to walk over the bent backs of several 'soldiers', using them as stepping-stones. The effect was magnificent. It wasn't too hard on the men's backs, as each step was momentary and performed at speed. On reaching the last one she was to launch herself into mid-air to be caught by her soldier lover and that was Jonathan.

Jonathan refused to do it, stating loudly and publicly that she was far too heavy for him to catch, without doing himself 'lasting damage'.

Shelagh was by no means fat, but she was of rather large build with ample hips and bosom. At five feet eight inches tall, she was not the sort of woman to pick a fight with, even if you were to discount 'the boyos from over the border'.

Ever the diplomat, I took Jonathan aside and patiently explained to him that weight had little to do with it, as well he knew. Dancing was about balance not weightlifting and that he wasn't required to haul her up from the floor, but merely to guide her safely down again.

It was literally, a split-second hold, before lowering her gently to the ground to embrace her. I think Shelagh, if given the choice between kissing Jonathan or a bucket of frogs, would have chosen the latter every time, but she was committed to the success of the show. She certainly had my undying admiration. I wouldn't have done it. What a trouper!

After several tries, they perfected the dance, but not without a lot of comment on Jonathan's part. I wondered how much he was actually entering into the spirit of the thing, as there seemed something very smug about him and I found myself wondering again just what he might be up to.

After each rehearsal, he just had to make a comment such as, "Had a big lunch today then?" or, "Do me a favour and leave the Mars bars until after we've danced tomorrow will you? You're getting harder to catch!"

To her credit, Shelagh tolerated all these insults in silence; secure in the knowledge that he was a pathetic little twit who would get his comeuppance eventually, if there were any justice in this world at all. The rest of the cast were becoming irritated with him too because after all, Shelagh was well-liked.

As the opening night drew closer, everything seemed to be going to plan. I thought it was going to be the best show ever. The only thing I was a bit worried about was my duet with Robbie. We did okay, but he was a much better singer than I was and I was a bit afraid of showing myself up. It was a very serious and poignant ballad, full of hope, that after the War all would soon return to normal; a song made famous by Ivor Novello. It went like this:

We'll gather lilacs in the spring again
And walk together down an English lane
Until our hearts have learned to sing again
When you come home once more
And in the evening by the firelight glow
You'll hold me tight and never let me go
Your arms will tell me all I want to know
When you come home once more.

The song brought the entire cast in at the end and rounded off both the first half and the 'First World War' theme nicely.

Robbie was to be dressed as an Army Officer and I, an ATS girl, very smart and formal, in complete contrast to the rest of the cast who had discarded their hats and uniform jackets.

On the penultimate line of the song, the word 'want' demanded a high top F, which had to be held. Being a soprano, I had no trouble reaching it, but poor Robbie struggled, so we agreed that he should mime it rather than strain. The trouble was, that during this song, we were supposed to be gazing lovingly into each other's eyes. That was fine, except that whenever we got to that note, he would deliberately go cross-eyed, making me corpse with laughter every time. I threatened him with all manner of retribution if he did it on 'the night' and although he promised not to, I really didn't trust him one little bit. By now, I knew him far too well!

***

The night of the dress rehearsal arrived at last. I told Shelagh that I was sure that everything was going far too well for comfort.

"You are just behaving like a first-time dance director, on the eve of a show," she tried to reassure me. "It's actually healthy to feel that way, gets the old adrenaline going."

"Well if the adrenaline gets going any faster," I'll probably have a heart attack," I said, not entirely joking, my heart pounding in my chest.

The first dance with Jonathan and Shelagh about to say 'farewell' at the station went like a dream. It was perfect, she in a lovely ankle-length floral dress which complimented her figure perfectly. Whilst he, in his uniform, looked wonderful, the trousers, incidentally just the right length!

They swayed and swirled in perfect harmony with the music. The train arrived on time, complete with steam and almost convincing sound effects, thanks to Sid the porter who was working like a beaver backstage.

I hardly dare look as it all built to a climax. Deftly, like someone half her size, Shelagh tiptoed lightly across the backs of the bending soldiers and leapt gracefully and perfectly into the air, ready to be caught safely in Jonathan's waiting arms.

And he missed her!

Everyone stopped, paralysed, as with a loud cry of alarm, Shelagh dived over the end of the stage and disappeared into the orchestra pit with a dull thud!

For a few heart-rending moments, the entire company held its breath in horrified expectation; then pandemonium broke out, with everyone rushing to peer over the edge. Bodies dropped down into the pit ready to render what assistance they could, as a stream of obscenities tainted the air from below.

Poor Shelagh lay spread-eagled and face down on top of Mick 'Boomer' Pashley, the drummer, (or so I presumed, as you couldn't see much of him, except for a shock of dark curly hair, amid the broken remnants of what had once been a very expensive kit!) Everyone certainly heard him though; he must have set a world record for the number of obscenities in one sentence.

Poor 'Boomer' had, until a few moments ago been taking a nap following the excesses of the previous evening's gig, or more precisely the wild party afterwards. He certainly had not been expecting an eleven stone dancer to land on the back of his neck from above and none too lightly either!

A jumble of willing hands and arms reached down to try and disentangle the pair of them, from where they lay in an almost comical position, had circumstances been different. Boomer's legs were wrapped around Shelagh in a desperate embrace of sheer surprise; a large cymbal, still vibrating, covering her head, where it had come to rest, like a Chinese 'coolie' hat.

The obscenities continued, louder than ever, as Jonathan rushed forward to peer at the carnage, claiming in that whining voice he adopted when threatened, that it was all an accident. And threatened he was as all eyes turned on him; wild, narrowing, accusing eyes. Wisely he beat a hasty retreat and disappeared.

The two bruised and battered bodies were retrieved from amid the shattered instruments, which were the only breakages, fortunately. They had both, by some miracle avoided serious injury, except of course for severely dented pride, at such intimate body contact in full view of everybody!

In spite of Lockley's protestations and apparent shock, I was convinced that he had dropped Shelagh deliberately and so emboldened by anger, I marched into the Doctors' residence, found his room and flung open the door without knocking.

He stepped back and cowered like a puppy which had just peed on the carpet, panic etched on his features, as I told him what a pathetic excuse for a man he really was and a cruel, dangerous little rat to boot. He did not protest as, turning on my heels I marched out again, watched by open-mouthed residents, relaxing on their day off, suddenly attentive at the sight of such a spectacle.

"It will be all right Shelagh!" I told her later. "It's sorted. He won't dare to pull another stunt like that."

"I'm sure you are right," agreed Shelagh, with a wry smile, "In fact, I'm sure he will not."

"Oh, God!" I thought, "She's sending 'the Boyos' round."

The following forty-eight hours flew by and before we knew it was performance night and the curtain went up with an audience packed to the doors. They cheered heartily at all the corny jokes, particularly the ones about the Consultants, who seemed to take it all with good grace and everyone on both sides of the footlights, had a thoroughly good time.

I crept up behind Jonathan, who was waiting in the wings, preparing for his entrance and with my face closer to him than was comfortable, whispered in his ear.

"Well now Jonathan," I said icily, "You may have done a good job convincing the others, but I know you for what you really are, so if you were thinking of doing it again, I would forget it or you will be very, very sorry." I must have sounded menacing for one so diminutive in height, for the colour drained from his face. Maybe, he'd had death threats from others too, as after all, Shelagh was very popular.

Whatever it was, had worked; the dance was magnificent, the audience erupting in applause and I breathed an enormous sigh of relief.

Now some may be familiar with the story of the 'Angel of Mons'.

During the infamous World War One battle, at which the Allies suffered devastating losses, it is said that an Angel appeared amid the carnage, to comfort the injured and the dying.

We used the story, making Shelagh as the 'sweetheart, appear in the guise of the Angel and Jonathan, the fatally injured soldier, continuing our storyline nicely.

I was particularly pleased with my choreography for this one, with Shelagh excelling herself and dancing it to perfection. Her long, flowing gown appeared almost translucent, performing a graceful and poignant ballet amongst the fallen, as she searched for her soldier lover. It was intended to be a very emotional moment.

"Break a leg, Shelagh!" I encouraged, in keeping with the best theatre traditions, just before she went on.

She held the audience spellbound, as she danced her complicated ballet around the stage searching for her stricken soldier and when finding him amid the bodies, rose up onto her 'points' with a joyous leap high into the air to come down by his side.

Jonathan had been lying on his back, legs apart, with his face turned dramatically toward the audience and was about to 'breathe his last'. I was convinced that is precisely what he thought he was going to do, as Shelagh landed heavily, and as she saw it, right on target! Her wooden, size seven ballet shoe came down right between his legs!

The tender moment was all Jonathan's as, with a scream of agony, he leapt to his feet clutching the assaulted area in both hands, and the sentiment, "You clumsy fat cow… You crushed my nuts!" is, after all, no way to speak to an Angel!

The 'lifeless' soldiers littered about the stage began to roll about with uncontrolled laughter, as the entire audience erupted in howls of mirth, tears rolling down their cheeks and cheering, all at the same time. Shelagh, to thunderous applause, curtseyed deeply to them, as Jonathan fled the stage still clutching his damaged 'wedding tackle'.

I'm sure the majority of the paying public thought it was all part of the act, but there were those prepared to swear, that the 'Angel of Mons' had tears of sheer joy in her eyes as she walked triumphantly from the stage. Justice had been well and truly done!

I went into my duet with Robbie with renewed confidence and vigour, now thoroughly enjoying myself. Robbie, on top form, sang his heart out and as we gazed into each other's eyes, I knew he wouldn't make me laugh tonight, because I wouldn't give him the chance. It was my turn! Taking a deep breath in preparation for that high note, I drew back my arm and jabbed an extended finger hard up his backside.

I will never forget the look on his face, as he hit that note, with perfect pitch for the first and only time in his life.

Chapter Ten

There came a soft knock on my door and Robbie's head appeared around it.

"Time for our talk!" he announced. "Are you ready? I nodded.

It had been two weeks since the heady night of the show and none of us had realised quite how weary its exertions had left us, wonderful though it had been, but now the time had come for more serious matters and our promised shared explanations.

"Your place or mine?" asked Robbie casually.

"Yours," I said firmly, stretching and getting up from the bed where I'd been lounging. It gave me the option to leave if things became uncomfortable. "Got any booze?"

He shrugged. "Of course, what a silly question."

"In that case," I said, "I'll bring the crisps… I mean potato chips." I was getting used to his vocabulary now and quite enjoyed using it.

The Nurses' Home was deserted. It was Saturday night and everyone had either gone to bed early or was out on the town. I hadn't wanted to go out. It was early December, the winter had set in and I was cold.

We sat cross-legged on Robbie's bed, facing each other, munching crisps and drinking beer from the bottle, completely at ease in each other's company.

I know so little about you, really, I thought as I watched him knock the top off another bottle, and somehow you seem to understand me so well. What is it about you Robbie that I find so fascinating? You certainly are an enigma. I bet there is so much more that you keep hidden from the world, like an iceberg below the surface. So am I ever to know the real you?

"Yeah, what?" he said suddenly, catching my gaze.

"Nothing really." I shrugged.

"Okay Pao!" he said putting down the half-empty bottle, "Life story. You asked me what I was doing here?" I was suddenly embarrassed.

"Look, Robbie, you don't have to tell me if you don't want to!"

Why the devil did I say that! I cannot believe I just said that. Of course, I want to know! Fortunately, he took no notice and went on quickly.

"I was at medical school in my final year back home, you know that and about to be let loose on the population… Oh, but still supervised of course."

I raise my eyebrows, nodding assent.

"I was working in a fantastic new facility near Austin, Texas; huge place, bang up to date! You have nothing like it over here, I guess!"

The Yanks always think they have the biggest and the best, I thought, raising my eyes to Heaven.

"No," said Robbie quickly, seeing this disdainful look, "This was unique Pao, a highly specialised burns unit where all the top surgeons from around the world were working."

"Why so unique? I was puzzled.

He was silent for a few moments, opened two more bottles and passed me one.

"Go on." I prompted softly.

"This place had been built solely, for the boys who had been brought back from Vietnam, horribly burned most of them, with injuries you just would not believe." He paused and drank another bottle of beer in silence; eyes fixed on the wall, remembering.

"There was this guy; I could never quite get him out of my mind. He had only one arm remaining and that was burned to hell. His hair was gone and both ears too, but he still wanted to live. He fought like a wounded animal because, after all, he had lost, he still wanted to live. Do you know the damnedest thing, Pao? It was our own artillery that blew his lower legs and other arm off and it was our Napalm that burned him. I figured that if we could do that to our own, then what the hell were we doing to the ordinary Vietnamese caught in the middle of it all, the women, the children and the old who were too weak to run. That guy has stayed with me since; there in the recesses of my mind, every waking hour, since that day. When they came to change those bandages, his screams were terrible. There was no pain medicine strong enough to knock him out and relieve what he was suffering. You wouldn't keep an animal like that, but still, he wanted to live. It was the smell of burned flesh you see and once you've smelled it you cannot ever forget it!"

Robbie paused and drank the rest of the bottle in one go.

"And did he live?" I asked presently.

"Nah, said Robbie, "How could he? Died peacefully though!"

The look in his eyes chilled me to the bone, as if there was a secret I was not allowed to share, that cold stare forbidding me to ask.

I tore my gaze away from his face, tears starting to form as I began to feel his pain. "Oh, dear God!" I whispered. "Robbie, please…"

"Don't worry, Pao. I didn't kill him if that's what you're supposing; the burns saw to that, but it took a very long time."

***

I listened motionless for the next hour, as he told the story of how fit young Americans like himself, had gone off to fight a glorious war when his Government had taken the decision to respond to the growing threat of Communism in South East Asia. He told me how their leaders believed that right was on their side; or perhaps it was that America had to be seen to be great. I listened to how those same boys had returned as men from that war, not as they went, but broken empty shells.

This was a war that until that moment had meant so little to me, save for the odd group of anti-war protesters on the news. It had, until that moment, seemed a very long distance away and I was ashamed, deeply ashamed.

Suddenly I wanted to do something, to go to London and yell alongside those protesters and to throw stones at the American embassy, adding my voice to the cry of how bloody wrong and futile it all was.

My generation had never seen war. Now, someone who I found myself caring for more each day was speaking about it with a passion I found impossible to ignore and as I gazed at his face I could see for the first time, the true suffering behind those eyes, as he went on with the story.

"All our lives we believed in America and that where she led, the rest of the world fell in line behind. We were the saviours, the protectors of freedom and if America sneezed, the rest of the world caught a cold."

Robbie's tone was sneering now, at his own country and its misplaced values, disgust pouring from him like an unstoppable torrent.

No wonder you had to leave Robbie!

"Uncle Sam!" he mocked, "protector of values and the great American dream where youth was put first. We were supposed to be the country's future! So what the hell was our Government doing sending that precious commodity to some paltry, far-flung corner of the earth called Vietnam, a place that half the world hadn't even heard of?"

What was this glorious country of ours doing? Proving a point? The truth was that America was getting its mighty ass kicked by a handful of Orientals and no-one dared to admit it!"

He looked at me earnestly. "I don't want you to think I am a coward Pao, but how can I fight for something I don't believe in? What does that make me in the eyes of the world? Draft dodger? Commie-lover? My brother is in 'Nam' and it's expected that I'll follow him when I'm old enough and have finished medical school. While ever I'm a student I'm protected."

"Some don't have that choice!" I said, regretting the remark instantly.

"Oh, lady," he said shaking his head sadly, "I had the effects of that lousy conflict rammed down my throat every day, as I looked at the broken bodies of boys only a little older than myself, so why them and not me? But you see Pao, war is at odds with everything I ever believed in!"

"Now please don't you go getting all religious on me." I chided, trying to lighten the mood a little and to my astonishment, he laughed out loud.

"Far from it Pao! I am trying to tell you something that only you will understand."

"But that's just it, Robbie," I whispered, "I'm afraid I don't understand."

He shrugged his shoulders and drank another bottle of beer in silence, then opening two more and placing them carefully on the dresser, reached forward and took both my hands in his, pulling me slowly toward him.

"My lovely Pao," he said, breaking into a grin, "You are probably the best friend I've ever had. All will become clear I promise; just bear with me."

My God, I thought, He's going to kiss me!

"It's okay," he said, seeing my consternation. "I'm not drunk enough yet and…" He stroked the side of my face tenderly, "neither are you."

That was his opinion! I hoped he'd had too much beer to consider adding me to his list of 'achievements', for in spite of what he thought, I was far too drunk to have put up much of a fight!

"You see Pao…" he began, his voice cracking with emotion.

There came the sound of heavy footsteps along the corridor stopping at his door, then a soft knock followed by an all too familiar voice. We both leapt to our feet, looking at each other sharply.

"Tissie! Bloody Hell! Tissie." How was this going to look? Here we were, 11:45 at night after lights out, lying on his bed drunk!

"One moment, Ma-am if you please," Robbie called, trying to keep his voice casual whilst looking round frantically.

"The closet, quick into the closet!"

"I bloody well will not!" I mouthed at him sotto voce emboldened by the beer. "What do you think I am? I'm not going in any bleedin' closet!"

"Then get under the bed or we're both dead men. You'll get us both thrown out of here!"

"What do you mean I'll get us thrown out?" I spat out the words in a strangled tone. "After all your antics, I don't know how you have the nerve to…"

"Shhhhhh," his finger went to his lips, frantically.

"Don't you bloody well shush me," I whispered angrily.

Without further ado, I was grabbed by the arm, wrestled to the ground and shoved unceremoniously under the bed.

"Shut up Pao!" he commanded, throwing empty beer bottles, crisp packets and ashtrays after me. "I'll get rid of her."

Dumbstruck at his insolence and with no time to object, I lay there motionless wondering how many other women he'd shoved under the bed when the situation called for it.

Robbie opened the door and let Tissie in. I hardly dared to breathe, as all I could see were two pairs of feet.

"Oh, Robert," she simpered, "I was doing my rounds and I saw the light. A little late tonight are we not?"

"Yeah, Ma-am, I'm so sorry. I was studying and I guess I was so intrigued by the anatomy of the reproductive system, that I quite forgot the time!"

She giggled coquettishly. Beneath the bed, I fought to suppress a strangled sob.

Be careful Robbie; don't push your luck!

"You seem to study far too much. A young man like you must have a little fun now and then you know. Have you not got a young lady?"

"Oh, Ma-am, I'm not really interested in girls at the moment, far too much work to do." I thought I was going to be sick!

"Oh, Robbie," said Tissie adoringly, "I do wish that some of my girls would take a leaf out of your book. The way they carry on sometimes makes me quite ashamed."

I reached out and pinched him viciously on the ankle, as he seemed to have forgotten I was there. In response he sat down heavily, flattening me against the lino. It had been a tight enough fit before without pressure from above!

Taking this gesture as a cue to talk, Tissie then proceeded to rattle on for what seemed like forever, about how hard he worked and how well he had fitted in. That woman could talk for England when she got going!

I was sure I was going to sneeze. The fluff under the bed was beginning to get up my nose. That cleaner needed sacking for a start! Desperately I pressed my tongue against the roof of my mouth in an effort to suppress the urge. It was only just working.

"For an impressionable young man," she babbled on, "your behaviour here surrounded by young women has been impeccable and I wanted you to know that it hasn't gone unnoticed."

"Why, Ma-am," said, Robbie, his voice as innocent as a choirboy's, "It has not been easy sometimes. I'm sure a woman of your experience knows how persistent young women can be. Take Paola for example. Lovely girl! Gone to see her family tonight I think, but in spite of all my efforts to be just friends, I'm afraid the poor, sweet thing has the most awful crush on me. She follows me everywhere like a devoted spaniel, bakes me cakes, offers to wash my socks and everything."

If at that second I could have got out from under the bed, I swear I would have strangled him with my bare hands, Tissie or no Tissie and to Hell with the consequences! With my one free fist, I thumped the underside of the mattress where he sat, only succeeding in hurting my hand when it caught the metal bed base.

"How very difficult for you," said Tissie pursing her lips, "would you like me to have a quiet word with her?"

"That won't be necessary thank you, Ma-am," said Robbie, "I'll try to let her down gently without hurting her feelings… you know how sensitive young girls can be."

"Perfectly," she said, "Goodnight Robert."

"A very good night to you, Ma-am," he said, ushering her out of the door. "And thank you. You are a wonderful person."

The second the door closed, I was out from under that bed and at him, furious and scarlet with rage.

"How dare you?" I howled. "What gives you the right to embarrass me like that? How can I ever look her in the face again? Robbie opened and closed his mouth like a goldfish, unable to get a word in. Barely stopping to draw breath I steamed on. "How dare you say those things, you-you son-of-a-bitch slob!" I wanted to be sure to use words he would understand first time around!

I caught sight of my reflection in the dressing mirror. Gosh, I looked really special, seething with rage and covered in fluff, fists balled, nails sticking into the palms of my hands.

"Pao, why are you so angry?" asked Robbie, in a voice calm and controlled, unlike mine.

"Why?" I shrieked not caring who heard now, "because it isn't true that's why! You… you… you pig… You wouldn't recognise the truth if it jumped up and bit you on the ass!"

"Oh, I get it!" he exclaimed with a grin, "maybe it wasn't so wide of the mark then. Seriously Pao, aren't you just a bit fond of me eh?"

"Don't you dare call me that. My name is Paola." I was hopping with rage.

"I think," he went on smugly, "that the only reason you are so angry is because I found you out and you are in fact, in love with me, game, set and match as you say here." My reply was a roar of indignation at his pomposity.

"How dare you? How bloody well dare you? Night after night I've laid in my room trying to sleep, whilst you and your sodding so-called 'achievements' made farmyard noises next door. How dare you tell me what I feel and just who do you think you are, some sort of god, obliging women to lay down at your bidding and open their legs? You… you unimaginable creep!" My index finger was only an inch from his nose and at that moment, I didn't know whether to kick him or poke him in the eye. "So don't you ever presume to be able to understand the way I feel!" He took a pace back.

"So you are in love with me Pao. I can live with that!"

With a scream, I hit him hard, full fist across the jaw, sending him reeling onto the bed, more from sheer surprise and loss of balance than any brute strength on my part. He rolled over and sat up, looking at me steadily, frowning and cocking his head like a wounded spaniel. "Feeling better huh lady?" I glared unable to speak, more shocked at what I'd done than he was.

"Now I wonder," he said, rubbing his jaw, "just which one of those voices of yours told you to do that, or did you decide all by yourself?"

I stared open-mouthed, rooted to the spot. How the devil could he possibly know anything about that?

Robbie got up and stood behind me to whisper in my ear. "Well, one of mine is telling me that I ought to slug you right back lady."

I flinched as he grabbed my wrist, spinning me around to face him and we struggled, falling onto the bed in a tangled heap, his arms tightly around me.

Then, his mouth found mine, with all the passion of a lover and I no longer wanted to fight him or resist. As our bodies merged in that most natural act, it was as though, this was meant to happen, from the very moment we set eyes on each other. There was no noise; no need for anyone to bang on the wall in frustration and demand quiet, but a gentle sort of love that comes from knowing someone as a friend first. That was not to say there was no passion, for there certainly was. Robbie was much more experienced than I was, but he was considerate and loving and made me feel that I was the only person he had ever made love to and I hoped that I made him feel the same.

That day, however, something changed between us, it had to and it was to change me forever. There is never any 'back-peddling' in a relationship when this intimate stage has been reached and once over that edge, then there really is no going back to being just friends. I didn't care if he had others, which he invariably did I am sure; he wasn't going to change the habit of a lifetime just because he had made love to me, but I didn't care. It was enough to want and have each other when we were together. There were never any promises, we had no need of them, as the only important thing was the here and now and not tomorrow, next week or next year.

***

"How long have you known," I asked, "about the voices?"

It was the next night; anger had cooled, perspective had been regained and there was now a new and lasting understanding between us. We sat on his bed once again, face to face holding hands.

"Oh, pretty much from the first time I saw you," he said softly, "with the cat. I knew that you were different, someone really special. There was light around you, bright and clear. I see lights… auras, energy, call it what you will. I knew at that moment, why I had come to this country, that there was a reason for all this and incidentally, I fancied you like hell!" He paused as if waiting for me to say something, but I played him at his own game. If he was expecting me to say his feelings had been reciprocated, I wasn't about to do that, not just yet anyway.

"Hummph," I frowned, remembering the noises from his room. If that had been his way of trying to make me jealous, then it hadn't worked. What was he doing… practising for the one he really wanted? I didn't believe that for a moment.

It seemed a strange pre-mating ritual, with the object of your affections in the adjoining room, able to hear every syllable of your antics, I don't think!

"Okay then," said Robbie, "more of my story, then yours. Only no booze tonight because we have got work to do." He got up, poured himself a glass of water and sat on the bed again. "My folks never considered it odd that I saw and heard things that other people didn't, because to them it was normal. I had the luck to be born into a very spiritually aware family and I wasn't considered different in the way you probably were. You see my Mother is a natural medium, as was her Mother before her. She is gifted and works all over the States, where things like that are not only tolerated but also freely accepted and even celebrated. Let's face it, Pao, Spiritualism had its roots back home so attitudes are bound to be a bit different. I was encouraged to develop the gift and at seven was sent to the Institute for Psychical Studies and the Paranormal in Austin. It had everything from your basic

Faraday cage to sophisticated electronics that would blow your mind. All of it is designed to eliminate chance and sort out who are the 'lucky guesses' and who has the natural ability and I was one of the latter. It's only by exposing the fakes and the showmen that the ones with genuine ability will ever be taken seriously. But all things considered, no matter how much ability you have, you still have to earn a living and fortunately, I had good enough grades to get into medical school and I was naïve enough to see why the two shouldn't go hand in hand. God, I did not know what I was in for! Oh, it wasn't just the Vietnam thing. It was when it came to things like resuscitating; then I knew I was really in trouble! In our 'high-tech' world, we have the means nowadays to keep people alive on machines indefinitely, no matter how old or sick. But is it right?"

"No, I don't think it is," I said, "not always."

"Oh, don't get me wrong Pao, I'm all for saving lives, but the problem was that I could see the other side of things. Old, worn-out people who had lived out their time, bodies and minds ravaged by disease, desperate for escape, desperate to move on. And there I was, pulling them back, delaying the natural order of things; not because it was right, but because someone told me I had to and it was against everything I believed in. I guess it got more and more difficult not to open my mouth and say so.

"I've been down that road a time or two myself," I said smiling, "Often best if you keep your thoughts to yourself."

"And what would you say?" he went on. "Look you guys, there are some of his people here who've come to fetch him, but you can't see them, right? He wants to go, so why the hell do we keep dragging him back? Come on chaps, give him a break and turn off the damned machine! Oh yeah, Pao. That would have gone down really well. They would have chewed me up and spat out the bits." Robbie raised his hands in a gesture of frustration.

"Did you ever say anything?" I asked.

"Only one time did it get me sufficiently riled to try and reason it out and the general opinion was that I was crazy. Got myself hauled up before the 'Chief' and was told in no uncertain terms that I was neither old enough or experienced enough to 'think', only to follow orders and to 'get on with it or get out'. Or at the very least to take a break and sort my mind out." He looked at me and grinned. "So here I am!"

I was beginning to understand. "And this is sorting out your life, eh soldier?"

"Yeah," he said quietly, "I'm doing it, slowly but surely, as you say over here, amongst your quaint country pubs, your green and pleasant land…"

"When it isn't raining," I interrupted.

"When it isn't raining! Amongst your fields, flowers, trees and pretty women."

"Well," I laughed, "That's one talent you seem to have brought with you, or were you a 'Casanova' at home too?"

"Oh, I'm just a regular guy Pao! It's just that you British are more reserved about that sort of thing… in spite of our conversation in the kitchen that night… believe me, there are plenty of guys back home far worse than I am."

I pretended to bite the back of my hand in mock horror. "In that case then," I said, rolling my eyes, "I just might pay America a visit one day and see for myself!"

"Wow! They would love your fiery temper," said Robbie, waving his arms around in perfect mimicry, before encircling me tenderly. "So long as you don't smash them in the mouth too often!"

***

Long into the night, after we had loved each other, I told him my story as we lay facing each other, bodies touching.

I told him about growing up and of the whisperings about me in corners, never to me. I told him of the frustrations of growing up different, with a secret that had to be kept and the gradual acceptance as I learned to cope with that which I had been given. And most important of all, I told him about Linnie; something I had never told another living soul, trusting him with my most treasured memories of a friendship that I would never forget. I told him how she had been lost and then found, never to be lost again and how my need for her presence was as important as breathing.

Robbie listened without interruption until I had finished, never letting his eyes stray from mine, in the soft glow of the winter moon which shone through the window.

"That is where we begin then," he said softly when I was done.

"Begin?" I asked sleepily, "Begin what?"

"You must begin to understand how to use it properly, this gift you have been entrusted with. Don't suppress it. You must develop and use it and you do that in the same way as you do with any other talent, by practising. I'm going to help you Pao, every step of the way. I truly believe it was fate that we met. Now I can give you something back for all you have given me."

"I can't think of anything that I've given you, Robbie," I said with a yawn, except sex perhaps and everyone I know seems to have done that!"

"You gave me more than you will ever know, lady, and I'll never forget."

"Well, let's just hope it isn't catching," I quipped, turning over, "and now I have got to sleep. God knows how we are going to work tomorrow."

We slipped into sleep wrapped in each other's arms, oblivious to the rest of the world outside our small private place.

Chapter Eleven

The Medical block consisted of three wards housed in sort of annexe, which stood apart from the main block of the hospital. The building looked as though it had been quite a grand mansion where someone of substance had resided in years gone by. Now the façade was a rather faded apology of its former glory. It had been converted many years ago for its present purpose and all that remained of its once impressive interior was a central ornate sweeping carved oak staircase, with cherubs at the top and bottom.

The building had been stripped of all its finery, to house the male medical ward on the ground floor, 'female medics' upstairs on one side and 'Private Patients', on the other. The ground floor corridors were long and there were rooms off. These had been converted into two, three and four-bedded wards and the occasional single to give privacy to the dying. The sickest patients were nursed nearest to the Sister's office in the middle. All the rooms on the south-facing side of the building had French doors directly to the outside at ground level.

Quite an innovation for the late sixties was our little Coronary Care Unit, also housed adjacent to the Office. It had a huge glass panel so we could see in from the corridor. By today's standards, of course, it was all very basic. There were a couple of ventilators and a defibrillating machine, to try and restart hearts if necessary.

By the door to Coronary Care was the cardiac arrest bell and if you were unfortunate to find someone collapsed and in cardiac arrest, you rang the bell. It was twice as loud as any fire-bell and was clearly designed to bring everyone running to help. The deafening noise, however, was such a shock when it went off, even to the staff, that anyone who hadn't suffered a heart attack at that point, would most probably have had one, particularly in the middle of the night, when all was quiet. I was terribly scared of it happening whilst I was on duty.

Although we had practised what to do, I had never actually resuscitated anyone for real. It was all very different when doing it on the rubber doll, which was called 'Resuscie Annie'.

She had a dreadful blonde wig and was dressed in a red nylon tracksuit. It was very difficult to blow with just the right technique to inflate her rubber lungs and of course, her lips were rigid. You had to pull her head back, first tilting her chin to open the airway. If you let go for a moment she didn't stay that way, but sank back flat again. Miss Appledore had told us that it was much easier on a real patient. It wasn't, as it happened. I never seemed to have enough hands for the job.

"If the worst happens, ring the bell and shout for help, very loudly," we were told, "and don't be afraid!"

They must have been joking! The whole prospect of someone dropping dead at your feet and you being the only person on God's earth, who stood between them and St Peter, was just a little daunting, to say the least.

An eighteen-year-old would never be put under that sort of pressure today, but in those days, you got 'thrown in at the deep end'. There weren't enough trained nurses for us students to be treated as supernumerary or 'mollycoddled', as was the word then. We were supervised, but equally required to be a productive part of the ward team and to act on our own initiative too.

So it was with gut-wrenching terror that I was stopped in my tracks one evening when passing the CCU window. I happened to glance in to see the man in the middle bed, slumped forward, blue around the mouth, tongue lolling, obviously in cardiac arrest.

"Shit," I gasped, instinctively thumping the bell, realisation hitting me like a brick that it was seven-thirty p.m. and all the visitors were around the beds.

Two women were sat, at the foot of the bed, happily knitting and chattering away to each other, oblivious to the fact that the chap in the bed had collapsed and was 'no more!'

I rushed in, pulling the curtains around the bed as I went.

"Pardon me, ladies, could you please step outside for a bit?" I cried almost upending the pair of them. They stopped knitting.

"Why? What's up duck?" asked the larger of the two, nonplussed.

I already had my arms around the man's chest, heaving him onto the floor. You couldn't resuscitate anyone on the saggy mattresses we had at the time. You had to put them on the floor.

"Just go, please!" I pleaded. "I'll be with you in a bit." My bedside manner left a lot to be desired. They stood and stared as I launched myself onto the lifeless body on the cold floor, thumping hard with my fist in the centre of his chest, the way we had been shown. It must have looked as if I was murdering him and why on earth they didn't try to pull me off him, I'll never know.

Please God, let someone come, I pleaded under my breath. They've all gone to supper and left me!

"You're on your own then!" said a gruff voice from behind me. "Now get on with it!"

I rolled the lifeless body onto its back, tilting the head, both my hands under the jawline. I took a deep breath and covering the mouth with mine, blew furiously for two long breaths. Nothing happened.

Chest compressions! I let go of the jaw and knelt at the side, placing my hands, one over the other, in the middle of the chest at nipple level, weight over my arms the way I had been taught. Pressing down rhythmically I counted aloud, "One-one-thousand, two-one-thousand, three-one-thousand," and so on, to ten. Quickly, I went back to the top end for two more breaths and then back again to compress. I was shattered already and I'd only done two rounds. There was no response save for a sobbing sound behind me. Doggedly, I kept going, adrenaline obviously in the driving seat spurring me on.

It didn't seem real! It was if I was watching myself do this. The part of me that stood watching, was calm, the other 'doing' part was panic-stricken.

I don't know how long it took, only minutes in reality, but suddenly, there came running feet and the sound of trolleys being pushed at speed. The male nurse on duty had been in the toilet and hadn't heard the bell at first. Eventually, he had rung the switchboard and the cardiac arrest team arrived at last, but they'd had to come from the other side of the main hospital and wait for the lift into the bargain!

Willing hands took over, safe, experienced hands which ushered me gently out of the way, as tubes were passed, oxygen connected, someone squeezed the portable bag and mask, breathing for the man on the floor. A senior anaesthetist took over the chest area and the defibrillator was brought. The patient was 'shocked' several times until his heart, still for so long was encouraged electrically into action and persuaded back into its normal rhythm.

I stood watching unable to move, my own heart pounding, face bright red, feeling as though I was going to expire myself. I watched, propped up against the wall, as the man began to breathe on his own and the redundant tube removed. He was placed back in his bed and propped up on pillows, now surrounded by intravenous drips. I saw his eyes flicker and open briefly to look strangely at the crowd gathered round his bed, as if wondering what all the fuss was about.

I turned, walked quickly back up the corridor to the outside door and was promptly sick in the fire-bucket. My legs had turned to jelly, face pale as I leaned against the stone pillar outside the door for support. I felt a soft hand on my shoulder. It was the senior registrar from the cardiac arrest team. He smiled at me kindly.

"Well done lass!" he said, peering cautiously into the bucket and grimacing. "Was that the first time?"

I nodded, still nauseous.

"Well, you did really well then!" he went on, "Probably saved his life. It won't be half so scary next time. Don't worry. Everybody has to lose their virginity sometime! Well done you!"

I couldn't imagine at that moment, I would last long enough for there ever to be a 'next time'. I was, however, wrong as usual. There were many, many more 'next times' and he was right. It wasn't ever quite so scary again!

***

Working on the medical ward was actually the first time that Robbie and I had been separated at work for quite a time. Perhaps Tissie was of the opinion that he no longer needed my guiding influence and had decided to cut him loose from my apron strings for a while.

We generally bumped into each other in the kitchen or dining room at some stage during the day and I no longer had to hammer on the adjoining wall at night, as we frequently seemed to end up together in one room or the other, easy in each other's company. I wondered if it was becoming far too comfortable, but quickly dismissed such a silly thought from my mind.

For Heaven's sake accept happiness while it lasts and don't question it too deeply. Enjoy it for what it is!

When I went to work on the Medical unit, Robbie stayed for a couple of weeks on the Children's' ward before going on to work in the Special Treatment Centre.

It was otherwise known as the 'Clap Clinic' or 'Crab Alley'. Female nurses were not allowed to work there. Maybe Matron thought that we young girls should know nothing about such things, or were of far too delicate sensibilities to deal with such 'nasty' antisocial diseases.

A senior and very masculine-looking Sister, who Robbie always swore, was a man, ran the clinic. She dealt personally with all the female patients and I'm sure that it took a lot of nerve for patients to even turn up in those days.

Sister May, as she was called, disliked Robbie from the first moment she saw him. He was sitting on the steps, which led to the clinic, eating a sandwich. In any clinic, particularly that one, a person often needs a bit of fresh air by lunchtime and he sat there happily munching away, oblivious to the string of phone calls that Sister May had received in the previous half-hour.

White with temper, fists clenched she marched menacingly down the steps towards him. Robbie saw her coming, feeling the very steps vibrate under him and he stood up quickly.

"You dreadful man!" she shrieked, "Get off my steps this minute!"

"Sorry Ma-am," he said giving a small bow of acknowledgement, "I really didn't know they were yours."

"What do you think you are doing?" she demanded.

"Just eating my lunch Ma-am, it's quite a nice day don't you think? Spring seems to me just around the corner!" She glowered at him.

"I suggest you follow it around the corner then, out of my sight. Such things may be permissible in your over-sexed liberal country." (She spat the last few words) "But here, I will not have it, do you hear? We do not advertise!"

Robbie looked at her, completely confused.

"I'm terribly sorry, Ma-am," and then asked tentatively, "what is it you believe I have done?"

"Done? Done?" she repeated. "You, young man are preventing all the female patients from coming in! Do you really suppose they want to see the cause of their troubles sitting there on the steps, eating a sandwich?"

"But it wasn't me Ma-am!" Robbie began, but thought better of further dialogue.

"You are a MAN, aren't you?" she bellowed, forming the word venomously, "and that is enough!"

Robbie ran back inside quickly, in case she was about to hit him, convinced by now that she was either insane or that someone had definitely been talking!

"She thinks that I alone am responsible for every sexually transmitted disease in the area!" he told us incredulously, at supper that night.

"There you go!" I said laughing, "Your reputation has preceded you once again."

***

The gentleman whose fate had apparently fallen into my hands, by way of his cardiac arrest was called Jack Morley. A few days later, I called in to see him. Not only had he survived my practising on him, but was sitting out of bed reading a racing paper. He looked up as I approached, folding it and placing it on the bed.

"Hello Mr Morley, are you feeling better now?" I asked.

"You must be Nurse Green," he said, "I thought I'd seen you before!"

"But Mr Morley," I began, "I hadn't seen you before, well… before…"

"Before I snuffed it!" he interjected. "I watched you come in that night you know lass. You said 'Shit' and then pressed that bell there. Then you chucked me on the floor like a sack of spuds and belted me just here." He touched his chest gingerly and winced. "You broke a couple of my ribs lass!"

"But you couldn't possibly have seen all that," I said, "You were…"

"A gonner!" he interrupted and laughing, pointed to the corner of the ceiling. "I was up there watching it all." My eyes followed to where he was looking and then back. "Saw it all. If you hadn't happened by, when you did, I would have been a 'gonner' and all! Them two silly cows of sisters o' mine, didn't even notice. I was here one minute and the next I was off up a sort o' long tunnel and it felt lovely. Then, all at once, I was being dragged back again and before I knew it, I was in this bed, wi' a terrible pain in me chest and me ribs caved in!"

He looked at me reproachfully over the top of his spectacles. I bit my lip wondering whether or not to apologise. Suddenly he threw back his head and laughed. You saved me life and I'm grateful. Just one thing! Tha' packs a right punch for a little 'un. God help any bloke that ever gets in thi' way!"

***

The days got longer, the nights lighter as spring gave way to early summer and time for another stint of night duty, on the medical block this time.

The best part of a year had passed since I had entered the profession, then a mere child emotionally. How we had all grown in that respect, the result of dealing with pain and sickness on a daily basis. We had all made the transition from schoolgirls to responsible adults in such a short time.

There are some things, however, that it is impossible to be adult about and that was my morbid fear of moths.

The entire frontage of the building was covered in Ivy and in this shrub lived the largest, most fearsome and hairiest moths it is possible to breed outside of the tropics. They were huge and woolly with black eyes and spots on their wings, leaving a dirty, dusty residue wherever they settled. To this day I hate moths, unable to stay in the same room as one. I know it's ridiculous! I am much bigger than they are and they are probably scared of me too and over the years I have heard every conceivable argument, telling myself to be rational and logical. That's the problem with phobias. They are neither rational nor logical.

Over the years I have had desensitisation treatment, relaxation and hypnotherapy. People have, in equal numbers been kind or have totally lost their temper with me. I have been cajoled and threatened, berated and ridiculed, all to no avail. I still scream and run in blind panic, as far away from the fluttery things as is possible to get.

In the daytime, I felt fairly safe, as all the awful creatures had found a roost after a hard night's terrifying people like me. They had often settled high up and didn't move unless disturbed. But if I should see one that had settled lower than ten feet up, I would harass the cleaning ladies mercilessly until it was removed. As far as I was concerned, the task took priority over everything that they happened to be doing. They usually humoured me, knowing that I had a genuine fear, though often casting their eyes towards Heaven.

Whenever I went to the toilet it seemed there was always one lurking there just waiting for me to sit down. I would cross my legs for hours rather than face my fear.

Phobias are supposed to be the result of a trauma early in your life, but I really couldn't remember anything like that happening.

A bat got into our bedroom once when we were kids. It clung desperately to the curtains whilst my Mother screamed for my

Father, convinced that bats would nest in women's hair given the opportunity. Annie and I were fascinated by it as I remember and not at all scared. The poor little creature had escaped through the window after my Mother had thrown her slippers at it and the way she was screaming it had obviously taken the opportunity to find somewhere quieter. All my life I have had a fondness for bats, so that really couldn't have been the catalyst for my phobia.

***

One July night we were sat in the office wrapped in our cloaks. Although the days were balmy, it still became chilly at around two am. I sat at the desk writing by the light of an angle-poised lamp, its beam illuminating the night report.

Suddenly a very large and particularly ugly moth with frilly wings hit the metal cup of the lamp, attracted by the light. Startled, I jumped backwards in my chair scraping the legs across the wooden floor noisily.

"What the hell is the matter?" shouted Mike Asquith, the senior nurse, who had been dozing at the time.

"It's only one of Pao's friends, don't panic!" said Mary, the auxillary nurse. "Shut your eyes again it's okay. She goes off like this now and again."

"Oh, God!" I exclaimed, "How I hate nights, with all these damn flying abominations about. They always land on me. If there were one hundred people in a room, the thing would land on me."

"They know you are scared of them," said Mary, trying to placate me. "They can probably smell the fear."

All was quiet for a while. The creature had clearly been discouraged, by getting its bits and pieces too near the hot metal and I began to relax.

Then I heard it coming. Big moths make a very distinctive buzzing sound and this one did, for it was the great-grandfather of them all! I scanned the room frantically and saw it making for the beam. I jumped up quickly to get out and it flew straight through one of the two holes in the top of my paper nurse's cap! Screaming, I tore at the cap, spinning frantically knocking colleagues in all directions. I could feel the moth fighting to escape the entanglement of hair under my cap, so firmly pinned on with hairgrips. Shrieking louder now and stumbling around, I tore desperately at my head in blind panic, fighting off poor Mary and Mike who were trying to help. Then I fainted, spark out on the floor.

It must have been only seconds until I came round and found myself looking up into the anxious faces of my colleagues, but it seemed much longer. They had rolled me over onto my side as nurses do, my hair was loose, the cap in tatters. Lying on the floor beside me lay the moth. I took a breath to scream again, instinctively. Mike held up his hands quickly.

"It's okay Pao," he said. "It's dead. Well, it should be, it's had my size thirteen stamping all over it." He ran his hand through his hair in a gesture of exasperation. "This phobia of yours is completely out of hand. Don't you think it's about time you did something about it?"

"Yeah," I grimaced. "Kill all the bloody insects and put me on days!"

I did, however, decide to give it some serious thought.

When I was in my thirties, a doctor friend felt he could cure me of the phobia, the silly man! In the intervening years, I had tried everything to no avail. It was as a result of my getting out of his car one day, whilst negotiating a roundabout at speed. His atrocious driving had disturbed a moth, which had been asleep somewhere in the car, and probably in fear of its life, had decided to make a move.

It hit the windscreen in front of me and buzzed. In a second, I had escaped my seat belt and out of the door, rolling onto the road surface to be narrowly missed by two cars and a bicycle. Grazed, battered and rather ashamed, I sat on the edge of the pavement, feeling sorry for myself and dabbing at my injuries with a tissue.

Faced with this spectacle, my friend had decided there and then that I must be cured of this affliction at all costs. What was the miraculous cure? He took me to the Tropical Butterfly House in Roundhay Park in Leeds.

Now my fear of butterflies is only just marginally less than my fear of moths, so I didn't immediately understand the logic of this idea, but he told me, "Trust me, I'm a Doctor," and assured me that I would either be, "completely cured or go raving mad." I warned him that it would probably be the latter.

On the journey there, I listened to a relaxation tape about phobias and we talked. By the time we arrived, I felt really relaxed and completely ready for the challenge. I told myself that I was thirty-five years old, a Mother and a wife with a responsible job where people depended on my skills for their well-being. It was time that I stopped allowing an irrational fear of a small insect rule my life.

So, after a final set of deep-breathing exercises, I was ready to walk into the controlled and finely balanced Eco-system, which was the Butterfly House.

The first thing that struck me was that it was very warm and humid, water dripping everywhere, like one imagines a tropical rain forest to be. With its tall shrubs and ferns, it really was quite pleasant to the eye. Gently taking me by the hand, my friend, whose name was Paul, led me further in, along a little path.

"Are you okay? he whispered, "remember to breathe slowly."

"Fine thanks," I replied, quietly. Several large notices said 'NO SUDDEN LOUD NOISES PLEASE'. Hand in hand we ventured in a little further. It really was quite pretty.

There was a bridge over the stream. It was made of wood with bamboo supports and clustered around the water's edge, several large tropical butterflies were drinking, their wings folded. I breathed a little faster and Paul, sensing this, held my hand tighter. I ventured to look upwards into the spreading foliage, gasping involuntarily as I realised that many more different coloured 'swallow-tails', were fanning their wings in the sunlight, clustered together on the glass above us, two or three deep in some parts where it was warm. Altogether there must have been hundreds of them. I turned to my friend and gave him a nervous smile.

"I can do this!" I said joyfully, and in that happy state, stepped backwards to admire the view, treading heavily on the foot of a small child.

"Muuuuummmmmmmmyyyyy!" came a tremendously loud howl of pain and indignation, "Mummy! Mummy! Mummy! She hurt my foot!"

With that first sudden noise, every butterfly in the place took flight, swarming around our heads in startled flapping.

My eyes widened in blind panic, blood pumping furiously to every muscle as the autonomic 'fight and flight' response was triggered into action and then I screamed.

My arms flailed like the sails of a windmill around my head, out of control, the normal parameters of accepted social behaviour abandoned. Blood rushed to my extremities and I ran back over the bamboo-bridge and along the path, scattering people left and right. The ones not fortunate enough to get out of my way were knocked over, as I headed frantically for the Exit and safety. I actually leapt over a pensioner in a wheelchair on the way out.

I lay on the grass outside, sobbing and gasping for air, anxiously running my fingers through my hair, unconvinced that the insects weren't clinging to me. Realisation dawned at that moment, that I was incurable and somehow I would have to find a way of sharing this world with them, whether I liked it or not.

The phobia was terrible. The cure was impossible.

It was a very silent journey home. I had made a complete fool of both my friend and myself whom, incidentally, never spoke to me again!

Chapter Twelve

After night duty on the Male Medical Unit, I was allocated to The Private Patient ward for six weeks. It proved to be long enough.

The building, of course, was the same, just a short walk upstairs. The décor was an improvement, with wallpaper in all the single rooms and the odd rug on the floor. The beds were the same, as was the bedding. I wondered what it was that the people who chose to pay actually got for their money.

Well! What they got, of course, was faster treatment and a degree of privacy, nice china, crockery and tea on a silver tray. In addition to all this apparent 'luxury', they got the tender ministrations of Sister Ethel Bell-Hamilton. She obviously was destined to be in charge of the private ward, as a double-barrelled name sounded so much more 'posh'.

She was a spinster and an awful fusspot when it came to her patients and their care. Every little thing had to be carried out in a precise way, every time. No time-saving measures were allowed at all. Thinking back, she probably suffered from Obsessive-Compulsive Disorder.

Sister 'BH' was a very upright woman, whether she was sitting or standing. When walking she always looked as though she was 'at attention'. I did wonder if she had been in the Army. Slouching, from any of her staff was not permitted. Her shrill voice seemed to follow me wherever I went, as she yelled at me,

"Stand up straight will you, young woman. Your posture is terrible."

My back ached terribly after the first few days from holding myself rigid whenever she was about. She trusted no-one with the care of 'her' patients and was forever hanging around outside doors to make sure that you were carrying out the most simple of tasks to her satisfaction.

Sister 'BH' always seemed to be there, but this occasion, she did go to her quarters, she handed over the reins to Staff Nurse Parker, often begrudgingly.

Miss Parker was only marginally less obsessive than Sister. She also looked quite old, probably well into her sixties and moved very slowly and sedately.

Both these women were their own worst enemics and certainly the way they carried on didn't do the rest of the nursing staff any favours at all. They created an unhealthy dependence in the patients and so when the occasion arose, that these two 'wonderful women' were not around, second best, as the rest of us were seen, was just not good enough!

Sister's greatest eccentricity came when any of her patients were unfortunate enough to die on her ward. She took it personally, crying for hours in the office and then having to be revived with bacon sandwiches and brandy from the medicine cupboard. On or off-duty she came to lay them out herself, no matter what hour of day or night. This was done with great ceremony and usually involved imbibing more brandy afterwards to calm her down.

No-one else, no matter how experienced was allowed to do dressings. We were allowed to serve food, give bedpans and make beds, in other words, the 'maid's duties'. We were permitted to give out the medicines, strictly under supervision and that was where Sister and I crossed swords for the first time.

You had to stand at the door of the medicine cupboard, holding a little silver tray on which was a clean linen tray cloth. On it was a china saucer with a doily, on which Sister, after consulting the patient's prescription chart, placed a silver spoon and on the silver spoon was laid the tablet. She would then tell you the patient's name, date of birth and room number and off you would go. Consequently, the medicine round took ages.

One evening I had been tidying beds in preparation for evening visiting time. In room six was an elderly ex-Colonel called Winterbottom. I bet he got ribbed mercilessly whilst he was climbing the ranks! He'd had surgery on his prostate gland two days previously.

This little gland which surrounds the neck of the bladder is a curse for many men from middle age onwards, causing problems with their 'waterworks'. Often it had to be removed and a catheter put in place for a few days afterwards, until normal plumbing services were resumed. The catheter was attached to a plastic bag to drain the urine away.

Old Colonel Winterbottom had been sitting out in a chair and had got impatient to get back into bed for his visitors. He had decided not to bother anyone and felt perfectly capable of doing this for himself. He rose from his chair and took a few steps toward the bed before suddenly being yanked backwards, forgetting of course, that the catheter and bag were attached to the other side of the chair. Only when he felt the excruciating pain of the catheter being tugged, did he realise he was not at liberty to walk off, without being freed first.

I walked into the room to find him kneeling in pain by his bedside, head bowed forward, rather like a little lad at bedtime saying his prayers.

Alarmed, I checked for any obvious damage and helped him back into bed. The catheter, which goes up the penis into the bladder, cannot really be pulled out too easily. It is held securely by a balloon, which is inflated with sterile water to prevent this happening. Still, he'd given the thing a tremendously painful tug, at the still-raw site of his operation only two days before. The pain was now firmly etched on his features.

"It's okay sweetie, I said trying to make him as comfortable as I could, "I'll get you something for the pain right away." The third-year Student Nurse told me that Sister had just gone off the ward somewhere and to go and get the pain relief myself.

"I'll come and check it for you," she said, throwing me the drug keys. We were honoured, being trusted with the keys!

"Now where are those flaming trays?" said Jenny, the third-year nurse as she dispensed Codeine onto a spoon.

"Oh, for Pete's sake!" I said exasperated. "The poor old chap's in agony! Do you suppose he cares if it's on a spoon, on a doily, on a saucer, on a tray cloth, on a tray? Bloody Hell Jenny, let's get it into him, he feels as if his bits have just been wrenched off for God's sake!" She laughed, ushering me away.

I hurried down the ward carrying the tablets balanced on the spoon. It was just like being back at primary school in the egg and spoon race, only I'd improved somewhat since then and the tablets remained safely in contact with the spoon.

I reached the door of room six and disaster struck. The swing doors to the ward opened and through them, swept Sister Bell-Hamilton. We came face to face and she glowered, eyes fixed on the spoon.

"Nurse!" she bellowed. "Just where do you think you are going with that?"

Quickly I told her of Colonel Winterbottom's unfortunate mishap and how his pain was so awful that there really was no time to find trays and saucers. I thought for a moment she was going to have a stroke, her face was so red, veins standing proud on her neck.

"Get back to the medicine cupboard at once!" she ordered pointing. "Whilst ever you are working on my ward you will do things according to my standards. And you won't be working on my ward for too much longer I think."

I couldn't imagine it possible for her face to get any redder, without popping an artery, but it did! I had suffered enough of this foolishness however and rounded on her.

"Sister…" I began, "Please will you listen to me? I used my judgement. The Colonel was in severe pain. I thought it much more sensible to get medication into him quickly and so relieve his pain, rather than mess around with niceties on this occasion! Isn't that what we are here to do, relieve pain?"

She did not reply but grabbed the spoon sending the pills flying and threw it on the floor with a stamp of her foot. I stepped back quickly. She fixed me with a steady stare of utter contempt and then pulling herself up straighter than ever, bawled, "Report to Matron this instant and don't come back on my ward again girl!"

I had the feeling that this was not going to be a good career move and it wasn't! Matron had not been impressed by my arguments either and I got the telling-off of my life for insubordination. It seemed that initiative was not to be recognised nor applauded, particularly when it came from a first-year student nurse.

I knew the score at once. Senior staff stuck together through thick and thin. I admitted defeat, and in spite of apologising, was promptly transferred to the Female Medical ward, with a black mark against my name. I was left to wonder if poor old Colonel Winterbottom ever did get his tablets.

After a week's orientation on 'Fe-Meds', as we called it, I found myself back on night-duty, yet again. They really knew how to dole out the punishment! I was beginning to consider myself one of God's nocturnal creatures.

The very first night we came on duty, one of the more pressing tasks was to 'lay-out' a newly deceased man. This was a female ward, but as the male medical ward was full to bursting point, one of our 'three-bedders' was now occupied by men.

It had been a hot weekend and everyone had been out gardening, probably doing too much digging when unused to it and hence, there had been a 'rush' on heart attacks. It was a grim task with which to start a long night. Val Carew, the third-year nurse-in-charge, decided to get the rest of the patients settled down first and then perhaps we could grab a cup of tea. Then after Night Sister had been to do the medicine round, we could tackle the job. After all, he wasn't going anywhere.

Later when all were settled down and the place was in darkness, we crept in to start the job, hopefully without disturbing the other two old men in the adjoining beds. They were sleeping peacefully, however, having had their night sedation half an hour before.

Pulling the curtains around the bed, we stood and stared at the enormity of our task. The body was of a huge man of some twenty stones, with heavily nicotine-stained fingers and a huge beer belly. Little wonder his heart had given out. We looked at each other and groaned.

"Pao, do you want to wash or dry?" asked Val. "Please say wash!" He was, in fact, really smelly. I gave in, holding out my hand for the flannel, which she quickly threw to me. I caught it deftly and we began.

It was hard work. A body is, after all a 'dead weight' literally. When you lift up an arm or a leg you have to take the weight the whole time, as it doesn't co-operate. The time came to roll him over to wash his back, so climbing onto the bed we just about managed to heave him over to face Val, after a lot of pulling and tugging. I looked at Val and puffed both of us breathing hard with the effort.

"Okay," I said, taking a deep breath and bracing my legs against the bed. "Let's roll him back. We go on three. One, two…" As Val started to push with all her might, a cloud of talcum powder, released by the movement billowed up into my face and I started to cough, letting go of him, as I choked.

I watched horrified, between gasps, as the strength of Val's push and the sudden lack of resistance from my side of the bed, caused the body to take on its own momentum. The weight, now unequal, it rolled and with a tremendous thud, fell over the side of the bed, pinning me to the ground underneath its great weight.

I tried to scream, but the breath had been driven from my body. Val scrambled across the bed and peered over the side. It must have resembled something from a Saturday afternoon all-in wrestling match.

"Get him off me!" I gasped, kicking my legs in a desperate attempt to extricate myself, shaking my head from side to side in disgust and panic.

Poor Val tugged furiously at the lifeless limbs, as I wriggled and shrieked whenever the air supply allowed. Suddenly engulfed by a wave of nausea, I retched, unproductively. That was fortunate. Unable to move, I would probably have drowned in my own vomit, lying there on the ward floor beneath a dead body.

Val lay on the floor and pushed with her feet to no avail, whilst I gasped every swear word I knew, several times, between squeaks of rising nauseous rage.

"Look Pao!" she said kneeling beside me, "stay there whilst I go for help. There is no way I can move him on my own."

"Don't you dare bloody well leave me," I sobbed. "Don't you go and leave me here like this!"

"I'll not be long," she soothed. I'll just run downstairs and get help. Try and lie still and breathe slowly and don't go anywhere, I'll be right back!"

"Where the hell do you think I'm going? I managed to croak between hoarse sobs. "Just be quick!"

I listened miserably as the sound of her footsteps disappeared down the corridor. With distaste beyond belief, I turned my head as far away to the side as I could, not daring to look into the lifeless face, inches from mine. It really could not get worse. Then it did.

Suddenly, I felt very warm around the middle, as I realised to my utter horror that his bladder had decided to empty itself, all over me. My sobs became a cry of sheer anguish as I finally lost control and screamed for help.

We'd only got to the washing stage of laying-out and had not packed or tied off the bits that we had needed to. "In future," I promised myself, "that's going to get done first and bugger the rules!"

It must have been two minutes at the most, the longest two minutes of my entire life, when footsteps came running and with a few collective heaves, I was at last free.

"Now get out from under that man Greeney!" the Night Superintendent said with a poorly disguised smirk. "Bloody Hell! If you're that desperate for a bloke, try and get one that's at least breathing next time!"

I sobbed, looking down at the wet patch on my dress with disgust.

"He's peed on me!" I wailed, before bolting for the bathroom to scrub my skin until it was raw, in a hot shower.

There were times, I really hated this lousy job and now was one of them. It was months before I could laugh along with the rest of the staff. After all, I'd had nightmares for weeks, usually involving being trapped in confined spaces, surrounded by decaying flesh.

Today, of course, you would be given debriefing and counselling, at the very least, but not then. Trauma counselling did not exist as such, apart from Sister patting you on the arm and stating that 'You are a nurse, now get on with it!" It wasn't accepted that we had feelings when there was a job to be done and anything so 'namby-pamby' as counselling came very low on the list of priorities when the annual funding was dished out. It was the accepted way of doing things; you did as you were told and got on with it.

So good a story, however, lost no time in circumnavigating the hospital with the speed of a comet. At least it gave everyone a good laugh at my expense and the standing joke for a while seemed to be 'What is green, white and wet and lies underneath a body?' (Ha, ha, ha!) I decided to laugh along with everyone else. It was easier and only years later did I realise that this was my debriefing and probably better that any counselling by so-called experts.

***

In spite of that horrendous experience on the first night, I came to love working on 'Fe-meds'. If any place, where so much illness and pain existed could ever be described as friendly, then 'Fe-meds' was just that. But there were rumours of strange 'goings-on'.

There are always tales of ghostly happenings in hospitals, by the very nature of what happens there and most of them are, without the product of overstimulated imaginations. Add to that, sick and dying people, impressionable young women and the highly charged atmosphere during the hours of darkness and you have the perfect recipe for the most explainable of incidents to be turned into something more. Usually there proves to be nothing more sinister than that. However, sometimes there is something going on for which there is no rational explanation and such was 'The Legend of Room 9'.

Shelagh had preceded me onto 'Fe-Meds' and had done a swap to Private Patients when I had disgraced myself with Sister.

"Pao, I tell you, there is something bloody funny about one of the rooms on that place!" she had exclaimed one night when we were out shopping.

"Don't be silly," I said, never taking Shelagh too seriously. After all, she came from a place where they still believed in fairies and leprechauns. In reply, she grabbed my elbow and steered me to the coffee shop. "Don't mock me," she said seriously, her eyes wide. "Didn' I tell you the truth about the ghost cat in yer bedroom, so I did?"

"Okay," I sighed, putting two cups of coffee on the table and sitting down. "Let's have it."

"Well, 'tis like this," she began, bowing her head in that conspiratorial way she did when telling you something she considered to be of national importance, "there is something in Room 9, so there is!"

"Something like what?" I asked.

"Something terrible and scary. Everyone I nursed in there, everyone over the whole six weeks I was there, died, every single one of them." I sat back and folded my arms.

"Shelagh, it's a medical ward! Of course, folk die. It's a single room. We put them in a single room when they are near the end, for Heaven's sake."

"Oh, No," she went on hurriedly, holding up a hand to silence me, "something is in there I tell you. One moment 'tis warm and the next 'tis cold as ice and once I fancied I saw someone standing in the corner, so I did. I tell you, Pao, I would not go in that room by myself again, I would not." She shuddered and pulled her jacket around her. "And poor old Richard Bradley was as scared as me and he has worked there for ages, so it must be true."

"He'd be pulling your chain." I tried to reassure her. "You know Richard, always on the look-out for a good story. Anyway, what is this? Send for Paola, the white witch of the west? Look, Shelagh, I start my nights on Monday and I'll let you know if I see any ghoulies, ghosties or long-leggedy beasties!

"Mock me at your peril then," she said, draining the coffee cup in one gulp.

Poor Shelagh! The creaks and moans of the old building with its equally ancient central heating system were enough to make even the most sensible and sceptical person 'spook' from time to time, when the shadows of night fell. Anyway, if there were anything unusual, I felt I would soon know.

***

Richard Bradley was a male student nurse, in the final year of his training. He was overtly gay and proud of it. "I'm as bent as an old farm bucket," he used to proclaim, hand on hip, striking the classic pose.

In the late '60s, gays were still regarded with some curiosity by the general public and it was accepted that they gravitated to certain professions; hairdressing and nursing. Richard represented the true stereotype, even before stereotypes were invented!

The nursing profession was extremely tolerant when it came to a person's sexuality. I suppose it saved them money in having to build fewer changing-rooms, because the 'men' were given a corner of ours, with only a curtain between.

No-one seemed to mind very much; after all, they were dead safe to be with and I loved Richard to bits, in a 'sisterly' sort of way.

The two prominent men in my life were at completely opposite ends of the scale when it came to gender. Robbie was casual to a fault, in everything, to the point of near-unconsciousness, whilst Richard looked nothing less than immaculate on or off duty. He really did not like getting those soft hands with their immaculately manicured fingernails dirty, insisting on wearing at least two pairs of gloves when he did anything.

***

Pamela Delaware had been admitted to the ward after vomiting blood. She was a forty-two-year-old spinster who lived alone in a cottage on a hillside near Buxton. For many years she had devoted her life to the care of stray cats; her bedside locker was adorned with various snapshots of them and she knew all her charges by name, despite having dozens of them. The years had not been particularly kind to Pam, probably due to loneliness and the somewhat harsh environment in which she lived; that particular part of the county being famous for its hard winters. The Snake Pass, which climbs over the Pennines into Manchester was often closed with the first few flakes of snow and could remain so for weeks sometimes.

Pam was grossly anaemic and looked it, her skin pale and almost translucent.

"Probably feeding all them moggies instead of herself." Richard quipped, striking his usual pose, seemingly incapable of standing 'normally'.

She had a lemony tint to her skin, as one gets with an exceptionally low blood count and it was really low, only 4 milligrams; the normal should be over 11 milligrams. It was hard to imagine how on earth she had actually been walking around with a count that low. With such diluted blood, her major organs must have been starved of nutrients. With severe anaemia, you get breathless, your immune system runs on slow speed and you pick up every bug that's going around, quickly becoming very ill, with no defences with which to fight infection. In actual fact, Pam looked surprisingly well-nourished so she must have been living on more than cat food.

Surely she must have been vomiting blood for some considerable time and this proved to be the case. Pam had felt that whatever was causing her problem would get better in its own good time, probably a belief inherited from her parents in the days when to see a doctor cost money and most people just couldn't afford it. What had finally brought her into hospital, was an overwhelming chest infection, contracted whilst her defences were down. It's amazing that even today just how many people are afraid to go to the doctor in case they are given bad news, when often with early diagnosis and treatment, even the more serious diseases can be halted.

Pam presented a diminutive figure hunched up in the bed; an intravenous drip attached to her arm, through which we could bombard her with antibiotics. She needed intensive physiotherapy and two of us nurses would tip and tilt her every two hours throughout the day and night, gently slapping our hands rhythmically over the bases of her lungs until she was stimulated to cough. This was to loosen the horribly tenacious mucous which clogged her lungs, so helping her to breathe. Going into her other arm was a blood transfusion, to replace some of what she had lost, slowly so as not to push her into heart failure. This blood had to be given slowly, because her heart had not been accustomed to working at full capacity and if it was suddenly expected to work harder then it would have been compromised and failed. It's rather like an old car that's only been used to go to church on a Sunday. If you suddenly expected it to do the Monte Carlo Rally, it would give 'up the ghost' after a couple of miles. The heart is, after all, a pump, the engine of the body. Pam would need at least six pints of blood to enable her body to begin to fight the infection. No-one gets that anaemic quickly, unless they have literally bled to death from a severed vessel in an accident.

It was suspected that she had ruptured a blood vessel in her lungs with all the coughing, but until her condition had stabilised a bit, we just couldn't risk taking her across the hospital to have further investigations. No such luxuries as portable x-ray equipment then, even if the somewhat temperamental lift had been working. So it was really important to watch the rate of that intravenous drip very carefully.

Today, we have computerised drip counters. You merely programme in the information, press the button and off it goes at the correct speed and rate and even bleeps insistently when approaching empty. What a doddle the job has become!

When this wonder of technology was first introduced we called it 'Robot nurse' and wondered if one day we would ever be replaced. The answer was a firm 'No!' It is hard to imagine a machine that can wipe bottoms and empty bedpans.

By the fourth night, there was a glimmer of colour on the tips of her cheeks and she looked a bit healthier, now without her oxygen for short periods of time, at last able to talk and sip water.

"Welcome back to the land of the living Pamela!" quipped Richard as we prepared to do the first lot of physiotherapy of the night. "We were wondering if you were going to join us on this set of nights or not. If I'd known you were going to be awake I'd have worn me Chanel No.5 sweetheart."

"Don't pay any attention to him, Pam," I said, busy with her 'drip'. "Smells like a tart's handkerchief, as it is most nights anyway." She smiled weakly. That was a good sign! "Come on Prince Charming," I said, "let's get on with some work and get that nice white tunic of yours dirty. It's dazzling me! See you in another two hours pet for your next workout. When we've done, you'll have muscles like Charles Atlas!"

Pam nodded, closing her eyes in a dismissive, "Leave me alone and let me rest' gesture and so we left, closing the door gently after making sure she had her 'call button'.

"Ooo, Charles Atlas! What a body." drooled Richard, as we walked to the next room, "I'd give me right knacker to meet Charles Atlas."

"You would?" I asked, eyebrows raised, not completely convinced that he had any to give away, "And he would most probably run a mile."

The male nurses' uniforms were much nicer than ours were and far more practical. Not for them the cumbersome white starched aprons, smart though they were and no caps, often impossible to keep perched on your head. There's were pristine white tunics and trousers to match, with coloured epaulettes at the shoulders to denote the year of training they were in; grey for first-year, light blue for the second and navy for the third-year. Red ones were for qualified staff and the colours corresponded to our Petersham belts. Sometimes, I thought Richard would have been more at home in a dress. I certainly would have preferred the trousers when bending, stretching and clambering on and off beds.

It was two and half-hours before we managed to get back for Pam's next 'physio', after no less than three admissions and a death and all before 2 a.m!

"Pam," I said, "first we're going to sit you up and lean you forward onto the pillows over the bed table and tap your chest. You know the routine by now I'm sure." She nodded at last able to participate a bit in the process. That was another good sign that she was feeling stronger. Better still, she was now tolerating 30 millilitres of water hourly.

"Big day tomorrow, Pam," I said, "cup of tea in the morning. You must be gasping for one." We Derbyshire lasses are fond of our cup of tea! "I bet it'll taste better than champagne."

"Oh, yes," she whispered weakly, smiling in anticipation of a long-awaited milestone that all of us take for granted.

Throughout the tapping and coughing that followed, Pam gazed lovingly at the photos of her cats. A local farmer's wife was calling in daily to feed them.

She knew them all by name and several slept on the foot of her bed. "Is there any room left for you?" I asked.

"Only just," came the reply. She clearly adored them all. And I told her the story of our tomcat that unexpectedly became a Mother, much to her amusement.

"I have an affinity with them," she said. "Don't much like people, but the cats and I understand each other." She paused for water. "Sometimes I wake in the night to find a couple of them actually sitting on top of me."

Richard grimaced. He was not exactly a cat lover. "Never mind," I said, "at the rate you are going, you'll soon be back with them and I bet they'll be really pleased to see you." There came a bright flash across my field of vision as I spoke, making me jump. I knew straight away what it meant. Oh, no, please not this one!

The job done, we made her comfortable laying her back against the pillows, freshly changed and plumped and after a final sip of water turned down the light to a soft glow. I stood for a few seconds more after Richard had left, looking at the sleeping woman, my face expressionless. Why do I need to know these things? Why can't I be just like anyone else in blissful ignorance? This is not fair! As I eased the door shut, something that hadn't registered before caught my eye. The door. It was Room 9! I left it ajar.

Quickly I caught Richard up at the end of the corridor and it was then that we heard it. A sudden and persistent choking sound was coming from Pam's room. Startled we both turned and ran back up the corridor, falling over each other as we went, anxious to see just what was going on within.

Poor Pam lay on her back, the pillows having been forced out of the way, her back arched in some obscene dance, head thrown back as she gurgled and gasped for air. "Get her up Rich!" I exclaimed, "She's choking on something!" As we hoisted her quickly into a sitting position there came an almighty bubbling sound and she threw her head forward and vomited like I had never seen before or since.

A torrent of blood shot from her mouth with such force and in such quantity, that it hit the opposite wall six feet away, pumping from her like a fountain, covering both Richard and myself, in our efforts to help her. As another red wave spurted at me, I instinctively turned my head away, my hair and the left side of my body sprayed with a fine mist as she exhaled.

I was too shocked to be horrified and far too busy, as her limp body fell back onto the bed as in one quick and practised move; I hauled her over onto her side, reaching for the suction. Raising her chin to allow access to the airway, I thrust the suction catheter down and withdrew half a bottle of pure blood in seconds.

She was not breathing! "Ring four twos!" I cried to Richard. "Respiratory arrest!" Her heart was still beating, but it wouldn't remain so for long if I didn't maintain her airway. Where the hell was all the blood coming from? Something big had ruptured something bloody big! In vain, I tried to suck it away until the bottle was full, whilst with my other hand, fitting an airbag to the wall oxygen. But as fast as I was bagging her, blood was pooling in her airway. "Oh, dear God! I said aloud. "Somebody help me!"

Then, at that moment, the emergency team arrived and took over. The anaesthetist intubated her via the nose and eventually, the bleeding slowed to a trickle.

Pam was quickly transferred to the Intensive Care Unit to try and save her life and there was nothing to lose now by moving her.

Only when the team had left, did Richard and I dare to look at each other, the two of us breathing as hard as 'not so fit club athletes' at the end of a marathon.

The room resembled an abattoir. There was blood on the walls, ceiling and all over the floor, the curtains blotted and smudged. Propped up against the far wall amongst the gore, crouched poor Richard, his back to the wall. Very slowly he stood, looking first at me, then down at himself. He was covered from head to foot in blood and other bodily fluids, his hair plastered down, red rivulets having run over his eyebrows and down his cheeks; once immaculate tunic and trousers stained heavily. He looked like a sheep that had lost its battle with the slaughterman!

Our eyes met and suddenly I laughed hysteria, sadness, pity and pathos all rolled into one. All I could see clearly, were the whites of his eyes.

"Fuck you, Greeney," he muttered miserably. "Look at me bleedin' uniform. Look at me bleedin' hair, will you? Shut up laughing, yer mare! I'll never get this lot out of me hair… Oh, Jesus, I'm going to be sick!"

"Oh, no you are not!" I retorted, shoving him towards the bathroom, "Or you'll damn well have to clean that up too. Get in the bath and I'll bring you some theatre scrubs to wear." I threw him a towel and shut the door. "Oh, and Richard," I called, biting my lip, "I think it's going to take more than Chanel No.5 to cover that lot up!"

***

The smell of human blood is very distinctive and once in your nostrils it is not easily removed. Not by washing, nor scrubbing, nor disguising it with perfumes. It only ever goes with the passage of time and only by taking the trouble to forget and do other things.

Pam's condition was stabilised that night in ICU, given more blood and taken to theatre a few days later for an examination under anaesthetic. The news was not good. She had gross oesophageal varices; large varicose veins, which stretched from the back of her throat to her stomach. If only a small portion of the tube had been affected, it would have been possible to remove that part and join it all together, but this was far too extensive, and very rare to be that severe. The whole oesophagus was a mass of bulging grape-like veins, which had now started to rupture. The condition was of course, totally incurable. They must have been forming there silently for years; an impending death sentence.

Two nights late, we found her back on the ward. Pam had come back to us for tender loving care and to die.

Her relatives, an elderly aunt and an older brother had come down from Castleford and although never a close family, they were nevertheless supportive and upset. Suddenly there comes the realisation, that someone, whom you may have taken for granted, is about to be snatched away, but as with Skye, all the wishing in the world was not going to change the situation.

Pam was dying from blood loss and heart failure and although she never had another devastating haemorrhage, her heart, unable to work with so little blood was slowly winding down to stillness. She died, clutching photos of her beloved cats to her breast, until at last the stillness of eternity overtook her. As her time approached, my hand was kept perfectly still on her head, so as not to disrupt the exquisite lights which swirled, rainbow-like around her, eventually carrying her on to a better place devoid of pain and suffering. Her relatives had already said their 'goodbyes' during the afternoon and so we laid her out, Richard and I and made her look lovely.

Before she was wrapped in the outer shroud, against all the rules I placed the snapshots of her friends, the cats beneath her hands determined she should not go without them. "Here you are Pam," I said softly, "I know you would want them with you forever." I stepped out onto the little balcony for a few moments of solitude.

It was a clear, peaceful night filled with stars. "Leave the doors open," I said to Richard, "and let the night in." We left respectfully to wait for the porter to take her away.

***

Mick Wilson, the mortuary porter looked the part. He had a long, solemn, 'undertaker-like' face, sallow complexion and pronounced nasal hair. He wore, as usual, his mortuary porter's long brown coat and looked as though he has just climbed out of one of his own coffins. Much more disturbing was his booming laugh, which tended to bounce off the walls. His face never moved when he laughed, no light in the eyes, no chin wobble, just that eerie fixed expression. If ever a man was suited to his job, it was Mick. He smelled of embalming fluid and gave me the creeps.

"One to pick up for the Ivy Cottage," he boomed.

Never should you name your house 'Ivy Cottage', no matter how quaint, as it is the universally recognised term for the Mortuary!

I smelled him before I had heard him or seen him and often wondered whether he had a wife and if she had grown used to it.

"Pam Delaware in single Room 9, I said turning to Mick distastefully.

"Ahhhh," said Mick, his expression unchanged, "The ghost room."

I shot him a hostile glance, "What?"

"Grey lady," he said in monotone, fish-like eyes fixing me with a stare, "comes and goes, she does so they say. Always die, them that's in Room 9"

"Don't be so silly," I said wondering if he'd been gossiping with Shelagh, "Of course they do! We put them in that single room to give them privacy toward the end."

"You'll see," he said, tapping the side of his hairy, hook-like nose. "Room 9… Always Room 9! In the dim light, his face looked even more cadaverous. "You two can go in and get her then, because I'm not going in there."

I was incredulous, at how a man who spent the majority of his working life in the company of the deceased in the mortuary, mostly on his own, could possibly be scared of ghosts. "Okay, Mick," I said, grabbing the trolley, "Come on Richard!"

"Stupid chuff!" retorted Richard as we opened the door of Pam's room.

Bright piercing eyes peered at us from the bed caught in a beam of light as we opened the door, unearthly beacons shining in the blackness. I gasped, startled but more as a response to Richard, who shrieked, wrapping both arms around me, one of his legs around my middle. "Bleedin' 'ell!" he screamed. "What the fuck is that?"

I reached for the light switch, trying to free myself from his vice-like unwanted embrace to reveal the reality.

Three very large, black cats reclined on top of Pam's still-warm body. They neither moved nor stirred, merely regarding us contemptuously, as finally, I managed to disentangle myself from the still trembling Richard and approached the bed slowly. They hissed in unison with jaws drawn back, ears flattened and heckles raised.

Richard whimpered as I knelt and spoke to them softly. "I know you came for her guys, but now we must take her you see, so it's time for you to go too."

I heard Richard gulp back a strangled sob, clearly convinced that I was insane and wondering or not whether to make a run for it.

Then suddenly, with a soft 'meow' from one, all three cats got up, stretched, jumped down from Pam's body and calmly walked out of the open balcony window and disappeared. Quickly, I got up and closed it after them, trying not to question too carefully where they could possibly have gone, given that we were thirty feet up, or have come from, for that matter.

As we wheeled the trolley down the corridor, Mick leaned closer than was comfortable, filling my nostrils with the heady aroma of embalming fluid.

"Told you," he said. "Room 9… Always Room 9!"

Chapter Thirteen

"Thank goodness," Shelagh said with a sigh, sinking down in the only comfortable chair in the kitchen. "I thought this day would never come. Two weeks off at last."

We student nurses were not allowed to take leave whenever the fancy took us. The whole 'year' had to take the same two weeks at the beginning of December in preparation for our year-end exams, which took take place the second week in January. It was probably a ruse to make sure we didn't have too much of a good time over the festive season and ensure that there was plenty of staff on duty for what was often a very busy holiday period.

"Are you going home at last?" I asked.

"The very second my last shift finishes, I will be on that plane, so I will. Honestly, Pao, I'm all in. I thought they only flogged horses!" She put back her head and yawned as if to emphasise the fact. "This is going to be the best Christmas ever, everyone's meeting up in Sligo and we're celebrating it two weeks early, just for me."

"Are the northern half of the family coming?" I enquired tentatively.

"Why, of course," she said looking at me curiously, "and why shouldn't they be? Well apart from great Uncle Willie, who's in the 'home', and there's Sean and Declan who are in the Maze, so they are! A terrible miscarriage of justice; did I never tell you?"

Only a couple of dozen times." I replied quickly before she launched into the story yet again.

"And what would you be doing then Pao? Are you going to be boring and stay here to study? Or are you perhaps going off with a certain man from over the water, yourself?"

"I don't think I'll be doing much of either," I said. "You know me, I'm not much of a 'swot'. If it doesn't go in the first time, it certainly doesn't do in the second."

"Is he the one Pao?" she asked, determined not to let me off the hook so easily from what was the real question.

"'The one what?" I teased.

"Don't pretend you don't know very well what I'm talking about," she said, getting up and heading for the door, but at the last minute, turning, seriously. "Don't get hurt Pao, please."

"Now why on earth should I get hurt?"

"Just don't get too close, that's all," she pleaded softly.

"I think it's a bit too late for that," I said with a trace of apology. With a sigh of inevitability, she left.

***

"Are we going to make that start on developing you into a half-decent medium then?" said Robbie the next afternoon. We had met in his room as arranged, at last with time to ourselves without work getting in the way. Robbie couldn't exactly slope off home for a couple of weeks. It was far too expensive and my parents had gone up to Scotland to visit my Father's aunt, who lived near the banks of Loch Lomond.

"It's not going to be all one-sided Pao, if that's what you think, I'm sure there are some things that you can teach me too," said Robbie.

"Oh, yes," I began, "spiritually or sexually?"

"Sorry!" he cut in quickly, holding up his hands," that must have sounded unbelievably crass."

"Well, I did use to call you my brash American."

"Why?"

"Well, let's just say you could do with learning the attributes of modesty and humility sometimes, Robbie." He looked bewildered.

"I don't think I'll ever understand you British."

"Never mind," I said. "Where do we begin?"

***

We sat on the bed and talked about Spiritualism and how the church condemned it because they saw it as communing with the Devil and all his works. We swapped stories of people we knew as teenagers, who had played with Ouija boards, believing it to be a harmless party game and how easily it was to have been sucked into something they really didn't understand.

"Did you ever do that? asked Robbie.

"No, I always felt that it was fundamentally wrong. Did you?"

"Yes, a few times, but you see, contacts you get like that can cause an awful lot of trouble. People who are bad here on earth don't suddenly undergo a miraculous transformation when they die. Murderers, swindlers and thieves stay that way on 'the other side'. They are put onto a lower level of consciousness in order to learn and repent, if that's the way you want to put it. It's these entities that a thing like the Ouija board, with its very primitive method of communication, picks up and they love nothing more than to hook people and tie them in knots. It gives them power that they would not have had otherwise, but as a medium, you are protected from all that nonsense. That is why we have guides and all my life I've only ever had one."

"Why have I got so many?" I asked puzzled, "and why do they come and go so much? Why can't I have just one?" Robbie nodded sagely. "Ah, I see. What you are really saying is that you want Linnie. She obviously meant a great deal to you."

"Yes, she did!" The friendships you form in your early life can be the most enduring and I had felt cheated when she was snatched away. "So yes, in answer to your question, I suppose that's exactly what I am saying."

"Your guides are given to you at birth and you really have no control over that. You see Pao, as you develop you get different ones who are right for your particular stage of development; in other words, the right tool for the right job. So if Linnie wants to work with you, I'm afraid she'll just have to get in the queue." I walked around the room, irritated and feeling it was all a bit unfair. Robbie's eyes followed me with interest.

"One of the first things you have to learn, I'm afraid is patience and methinks perhaps, that is not one of your strong points, milady," said Robbie giving a small bow and a touch of the forelock. I responded by throwing a pillow at him, which he caught deftly. "Be assured of one thing though, Pao, if you really need her and I mean really, really need her, then she will come, I know. In the meantime, you have to take the time to get to know your guides for, after all, they know you inside out and have done so for a long time. It's a very privileged relationship. We come into contact with vulnerable people at difficult times in their lives. It's only when you've lost someone, do you realise that perhaps your long-held beliefs just don't have the answers you need. That's when they come to us."

"And, it's a hell of a responsibility," I said sitting down again.

"But a responsibility you are capable of, otherwise you wouldn't have been given it. They'd have given up on you long ago. There are a lot of misguided individuals in this game who think they have it and they don't and there are the fakes of course, who see a means of making a quick buck. The bereaved are easy targets for the unscrupulous, because most people would give anything for a few moments more with a loved one, whatever the cost. They are desperate for proof that life goes on."

"Which is why real mediums shouldn't charge. "I said, nodding. "Abuse the gift and it will be taken away."

Tenderly he placed his arms around me. "Which is why when someone has a gift as powerful as yours, you must use it for good. How you do that will be up to you, but it was given for a reason. Think how much poorer this world would be if Picasso had only used his gift to paint hen-houses and picket fences. Go for it and use it to the full honey but always remember the rules, compassion, accuracy and responsibility for we hold raw emotions in our hands. Now get comfy, relax and let's see what you are capable of shall we?"

I kissed him softly on the mouth and lay on the bed, head on a soft pillow. Breathing slowly and deliberately as I had learned by trial and error over the years to induce a state of deep relaxation I waited for calm to settle around me like a silken cloak. Robbie settled beside me, his face close enough to my cheek for me to feel his gentle breathing. When he spoke it was softly. "Don't try to concentrate, allow your mind to lead you where it will, relax, use my voice as a focus if you want to and when you are ready tell me what you see." There was nothing. Patience, have patience now. I waited. "Nothing but total darkness," I said twitching with frustration.

"Patience should become your mantra," whispered Robbie close to my ear. "Relax and don't try so hard. Let them come to you, not the other way round. Try to open a channel that they can use." With a deep sigh, I began afresh, imagining I was once again lying amongst the flowers in 'High Meadow', on a balmy summer's day, seeing the scene through the eyes of a child and noticing it's simple pleasures as if for the first time.

"Now," asked Robbie's soft voice, "what do you feel?"

"Lovely!" I whispered sleepily from the dream-like state that had overtaken me, "soft, warm and safe."

"Good, now allow your mind to go a little deeper into relaxation." He paused for a few moments. "Tell me what you can hear."

"My breathing, heartbeat, a train in the distance. I'm so sleepy," I yawned and shuffled.

"Are you too warm Pao?"

"A bit."

"That's okay. Sometimes when 'spirits' come close, they bring a surge of energy. It will pass in a moment or two. "Do you see anything?"

"A light," I said, a little louder, "I see a light."

"What sort of light? Can you describe it?"

"It began as just a pinprick of blue, now it's brighter, spreading outwards, swirling blue, the most beautiful blue."

"Good," said Robbie softly. "When you see blue you know you are safe and protected. Blue is for healing and is the colour that comes with your guide and you know then that it is safe to go on. Let it swirl around you."

The well-being that I felt at that moment was incredible and I would have gladly stayed there forever. It was as though all the troubles of the world could be solved in that instant. The light dissipated outwards and suddenly a burst of vibrant colours exploded before me, like fireworks in the night sky, before settling to a recognisable scene. Robbie's voice drifted somewhere in the distance as I watched and listened like an eavesdropper; a sightseer on some spectacular jaunt.

"Gosh, Robbie, this is wonderful. There are trees and a forest, so green and dense, but it's not here in England. It's somewhere very far away. I feel as though I can reach out and touch the leaves, banana fronds! It's a tropical forest and it's dripping with rain… so beautiful, it's…" There was a sudden flash and the image was gone, but my eyes stayed closed, longing for its return. Although I couldn't see his face, I was sure that Robbie was smiling. "Didn't last long I'm afraid," I said apologetically.

He had begun to answer when I heard a sound and I held up my hand to silence him, my head turning toward the direction from which it came.

"What is it, Pao?"

The throbbing sound came closer, growing in intensity, increasing in volume until I wondered why the room wasn't shaking. I looked up, alarmed, the sound changing to a drone and dying and I realised that it was not in the sky at all, but inside my head.

"Oh, that's better," I exclaimed with a shake of my head to clear it. "Fill," I said, after a pause.

"Fill what?" said Robbie, helping me into a sitting position, "Or Phil who?"

"Don't know, Robbie," I said. "That's all I got. Just the word, 'Fill'. I could see it in front of my face, very clearly."

"My brother is called Phil," said Robbie, almost as an aside comment.

"Oh, no you don't understand, it's not that kind of Phil, not anyone's name."

"What then? He asked. "If you don't know, ask for more information, broaden the thought and think around it. Sometimes you have to sort out the…"

"Wheat from the chaff? I interrupted, the words of an old lady suddenly making sense. "Here, hand me a piece of paper and I'll write it down as I saw it, if it helps." Quickly I scribbled on the paper and handed it to him.

"Okay, I think that's quite enough for today," said Robbie, handing me a can of cola after I'd finished stretching and yawning. "We'll do a little more each day and see how we…" Robbie stopped suddenly and stared at the slip of paper in his hand.

"That's not 'fill' Pao, that's F-one-eleven, see you put dashes between the letters. Now I see. An F-one-eleven's an aeroplane, a low-level bomber. That would have been the noise you heard, the noise of the engines." I looked at him triumphantly, but saw only unease in his eyes. "What's wrong Robbie?"

"Nothing at all," he said, the smile returning, kissing my throat in the preliminaries of lovemaking, only I knew better.

***

We worked on my 'progression' each day for the next two weeks. I learned quickly from Robbie, drawing on his wealth of experience. I learned to question everything and never to take anything at face value. In all of the learning process however, two things became predictable. The first was that afterwards we would end up in bed, wrapped in each other's arms and the second was that I would always somehow find myself deep within that same green tropical forest, with the soft, warm rain falling.

***

There was a knock and Robbie's face appeared round the door. Christmas had come and gone and here we were, almost at the end of our first year of Nurse Training, older, wiser and allegedly more mature. Exams were over and there were now only the results to worry about after which the whole process would begin again, the only difference being, a different coloured belt to denote that we were now in our second year.

"Hi, Robbie," I said, getting up from my accustomed reading position on the bed. "What's up?" He shut the door but did not sit.

"I've got something rather important to tell you, Pao."

"Don't tell me! Your premium bonds have come up, you are now unbelievably rich and intend to keep me in the manner to which I could rapidly become accustomed."

"No," he hesitated.

"You didn't get someone pregnant, did you?" I said, feigning a fit of the vapours.

"Pao, please listen," the seriousness of his expression making me stop. "What is it?"

"I'm going home!"

If someone had hit me with a brick it couldn't have had more impact. "Oh, Robbie!" I managed to say it before the tears came and we held each other. "I'm sorry, Robbie, I guess it was a shock, I wasn't expecting it, not yet somehow."

How could he go? I loved him and I said I would not fall in love with him, but God help me, I had! I liked to think that somehow his own way, that he loved me but we had never told each other, not said the actual words, not even at the height of passion. I felt as though I had been punched somewhere around the middle and I felt sick, my head whirling in the turmoil of so many different emotions.

"Robbie, why are you going?" He looked at the floor not answering and as we sat side by side on the floor of my room, I traced patterns on the surface of the worn carpet with my finger, absently, just for something to do with my hands.

"I guess that means you've resolved what you came here to do," I said eventually. "Or are you unbelievably homesick for those beautiful sunsets you are always ranting on about?"

"I'm sorry Pao, it's just that now I know where I'm going at last. The two halves of my life have come together and they can exist side by side now. I can't begin to tell you what a big part you played in making that happen.

"Me? What have I had to do with it?" I asked, not really believing him.

"Oh," he sighed sadly, "by trying to see beyond the façade and accepting me as the far from perfect person I am and by taking the time to show me that I wasn't God's gift to women."

"Do you have any idea how much I-I-I… c-care for you, Robbie," I stammered, choking back the tears again, trying not to say what I really felt.

"I know. Please don't say the words Pao don't make it any harder, please."

I wanted to scream, to hit him and to hold him and to yell.

What about me? Where does that leave me? You may have resolved your life but what about mine? Don't I matter? But I didn't say any of it.

"Don't say it Pao!" he said again, "We have something that is far too precious to spoil."

"Sounds like crap to me! I exclaimed, stung.

"Don't get hurt Pao." I heard Shelagh's words ring in my ears along with all the other subtle warnings that I had chosen to ignore. Turning to face him I forced a smile. "When are you going?"

"Friday," he said softly, not taking his eyes from my face.

Four days!

"I was really lucky to get a berth, from Liverpool. You will come and see me off won't you Pao?" I failed to see how I could bear to do that.

"What will you do Robbie? Go back to medicine?"

"There's something important I have to do first." He placed his fingers on my lips to prevent me speaking. "Don't ask, Pao, please. I'll write and tell you all about it!"

"Tell me now!" I demanded, slighted and confused at his secrecy, even now when so much had passed between us.

"When I get home," he said, "I promise."

"Please make sure that you do, after all, we've meant to each other, Robbie. For friendship if for nothing else." For a few minutes, we stood in silence, holding hands and looking into each other's faces.

"There's something else I have to tell you, Pao. It's about you. You won't find the love of your life until you are older," he said pointedly, "much older."

Funny, I thought that I had!

"Oh, I'm not saying that you'll not find what you think passes for it, but don't go searching, because you'll only be wasting your time. One day, when the time is right, he'll come looking for you." He paused and took a deep breath, blowing the air out slowly. "Oh, honey, I hope you're strong!"

"You know I am," I said, looking at my fingernails, "and stubborn!"

"Well, you'd better be, gal, because this guy will steal your heart and soul."

Someone has already stolen those. A sly American thicf who came in the night!

"There are those that would say the Devil's already had those," I quipped, trying to make an effort at humour.

Nothing can surely ever hurt this much again!

"Well then," he went on, "just as well we know the truth. We only work with the help of God or whatever name you choose to call him, but before you can find true happiness Pao, this guy's gonna tear you apart. It's necessary and will be worth it, so remember that when it looks dark out there.

"And what sort of a lousy, sonofabitch set-up is that?" I cried angrily.

"A damn good one. You have to hurt like hell sometimes, to appreciate it when it happens for real. That way you make damn sure you never make the same mistake again."

"But is it worth all the trouble and heartache?" I pleaded, tears once again flowing freely. He brushed them away with a sweep of his thumb.

"Oh, it will be! When it comes, it sure will be! From that day you had better hang on to your hat. Besides all that, you have got all the potential to be a great medium, but the rest is up to you now. You have work to do."

"I know that," I said.

"Then go out there and tell the rest!"

"The rest don't always want to hear."

"Then do it more subtly," said Robbie, "You don't have to be like the Jehovah's 'whatsits' and go door to door… sing it out if you must!"

"I would have thought having had first-hand experience of my voice, you wouldn't want to inflict that on society," I said, calmer now.

"Then, write about it. I know you can do that. Tell them we're not unusual Pao, that we're just ordinary people with a bit of extra insight that's all. Tell them we're not strange. We work, play, love, make mistakes and chase women just like everybody else. We've just developed an extra talent that's all. Make me a promise that you'll do it."

"I'll do it one day," I promised.

"I know you will." He nodded. "Not everyone works in the way I do; we all have to find our own way. Gifts are given in so many different wrappings. Don't waste them! Tell the story, tell it all baby. Oh, and by the way, look out for the next one who calls you 'baby', then you can be sure that love is for real. That is how you will know."

***

We had a wonderful, drunken, loud and very late party, the evening before Robbie left, everyone sorry to see him go. He had lit up our lives for a while, some more so than others and had managed to break a few hearts along the way, whilst leaving serious dents in a few others. But beneath his wild philandering, walked one very special person indeed and I had been allowed to see that part not privy to others. I was devastated at his leaving.

After the party, when everyone else had gone to bed, we sat in the kitchen just before dawn, holding hands across the scrubbed pine table. Scraping back the chair noisily, Robbie got up. "Cocoa?"

"What the hell's cocoa?" I asked in my best American accent.

"Oh, I think you call it chocolate!" He mimicked my English voice perfectly.

"Well then," I said unable to look up from the table, "If it's no trouble, I'd love some." He opened the fridge.

"Bags packed?"

"Yes, Ma-am! Come and see me off, Pao, please. Come with all the others."

"I don't think I can," I said still unable to look up from the table.

"Please don't forget me, Pao!" I looked at him finally, my eyes brimming with tears.

"Could I ever?"

When you meet the love of your life, you'll remember me and all the things we've said tonight."

"You're full of bullshit," I said, swallowing hard.

"You know I'm not," he whispered, "not when it's as important as this. Be happy whenever you think of me, Pao."

"Get the hell out of here before I cry," I said firmly. He held my hands tightly in his.

"Friends forever?"

"Friends forever! Goodbye, Robbie." And with that, he kissed my forehead and left.

***

That last night I could never have imagined how I could exist without him. That's love for you! We had shared a wonderful relationship in our all-too-short time together and the separation hurt, not just emotionally but physically. Mothers who have lost infants say it; people who have lost their long-term partners say it. It's called 'empty arms syndrome', the physical longing for that person, to touch and to be touched in return. But life goes on.

I did go to Liverpool to see Robbie off, despite what I said in the kitchen that last night. Shelagh, feeling she knew what was best for me, had all but pushed me onto the train. There was a small delegation going to wish him well or maybe, in some cases, to make sure he went! Having other people around was strangely comforting, removing the need to find those final parting words, over and above those which had been already said.

Brightly coloured streamers stretched from the rail of the SS Flavia to the shore. I clutched the end of my red streamer tightly as the ship slowly pulled away from the dock, Robbie's face easily distinguishable amongst the waving crowd on deck, his dark curly head standing out against the white livery of the ship. The streamers grew taught, our eyes locked together and he gave a wave which I knew was for me alone. Then, the link between us snapped, leaving me clutching one end tightly, the other trailing in the dark green oily water of the dock. Long after the ship could no longer be seen, I stared at the still water mesmerised, not wanting to let go.

A soft hand was placed on my arm. It was Shelagh, who had kindly kept the others away, dispatching them off to have a cup of coffee, whilst she watched me from a respectable distance, presumably in case I decided to throw myself in. But nothing was actually further from my mind. Solitude was what I needed and my dear friend had seen that and supplied it.

"Time to go, Pao," she said quietly, the lilting voice comforting. "Time to open another door now, so it is."

"I haven't closed this one yet." I murmured.

"Then leave it ajar for a little while yet and then when you are good and ready…" her voice trailed off. "Come now, time to go home."

***

When someone like Robbie moves on, they leave a huge gap in your life at first, but it's amazing how soon the general flotsam and jetsam of life move in to fill it.

I missed Robbie, his love, companionship and his sense of fun. I missed his way of talking, his friendship and his physical presence in my life. I wondered constantly about him, where he was, if he was settled and if he had found happiness. Above all, I was curious about his mystery mission and waited impatiently for the promised letter of explanation. It never came.

Oh, well, I thought philosophically, forgotten about me already I suppose now you are back amongst all those willing American girls again! A couple of months down the line and I was able to look at the situation from a calmer place. I wondered if he was still climbing up to the ridge of an evening to look at the sunsets.

Stop it! What an incurable romantic you are Paola Green!

***

One evening, a few weeks later, it was my turn to cook supper and I was busy in the kitchen. "Come on you lot, get your books off the table if you want to eat." I ordered, waving a wooden spoon. The large kitchen table was always a popular place to do written work, as space was limited in our rooms. Shelagh had just offered to set the table, when Tissie came in. "Ah, Nurse, there you are. I have been trying to catch you all day." She bustled across the kitchen to where I was busily stirring pasta sauce. "This letter came for you."

I took it with a buzz of excitement as I read 'Par Avion'. Airmail with an American postmark!

"About time," I said, "thought you'd forgotten how to write Robbie! Now I suppose we are at last going to be treated to the details of his exploits since he went home."

"Come on Pao! For Heaven's sake open it," begged Shelagh, obviously desperate for the juicy bits, along with everyone else. I held the letter high above my head, taunting them. "Mine," I said emphatically, "and I'll open it only when you've all backed off to a respectable distance."

With deliberate slowness, I settled myself on top of the boiler. It was spring, but the nights were still cold. I tore open the thin paper carefully and frowned disappointedly. "It's not from Robbie," I said aloud. "It's not his writing."

Everyone suddenly lost interest and carried on with the business of supper. Tucking my feet under me, I went back to the letter.

'Dear Paola…' The handwriting was unmistakably a woman's, flowing and elegant, pretty script which should have said pleasant things. 'Dear Paola, I read again, 'Although we never met, I feel that I know you quite well. My son Robbie spoke of you so often and of your special friendship. He loved his time in England and it was obvious that you meant a great deal to him. He called you his 'beautiful English rose' and so I am sure you will understand that it is with so much pain in my heart that I have to tell you this my dear…'

Staring at the words, shocked beyond belief, I stifled a cry.

Robbie was dead!

I looked around. It was as if the world had become a film playing in slow motion and one in which I played no part. My eyes were fixed on the flimsy piece of paper as it fluttered slowly to the floor, like a leaf in autumn. I neither saw nor heard anything, as heads turned and cutlery fell, nor Shelagh bending to pick up the letter. Numbness crept around me like a fog, an impenetrable blanket of cold, misty darkness.

Dead! No. How could he be? It had to be a mistake, some ghastly mistake! Robbie so fit, so vibrant and healthy. Yes, that's it, an error for which there has to be some simple explanation. Perhaps I'll wake up in a minute!

Somewhere far away, I heard Shelagh reading, to a silent and disbelieving audience and I heard the words again, as I sat alone and dazed on the boiler in my own little world. For what seemed like a very long time I sat there staring.

Robbie had gone home and immediately volunteered for Vietnam, for whatever reason I guessed I should never know. He had hated war, so why on earth should he have wanted to face it head-on? What had he said that night in the sluice room? "I have to reconcile something in one part of my life so that I can get on with the rest of it. So why had he gone off to face what he feared most and to hell with the consequences? But why, Robbie, why?

The only certain thing was that he had enlisted of his own free will and six weeks later had been returned in a body bag, his plane having been shot down over the jungle near Da Nang. I choked back a panic-stricken sob, suddenly remembering, my mind racing back to that tropical forest where I went during our shared evenings and once again heard the whine of the engines. Oh, God! I didn't want to know if that was the one. Was it his plane, his forest? Had I foreseen his death and had he realised it too? Did he know and is that why he had to go? I remembered the strange look in his eyes when we first recognised, that what I was seeing was an aircraft.

***

Suddenly I felt as responsible for his death, as the 'Vietcong' who had fired the anti-aircraft missile that had killed him.

The sense of shock was immeasurable, unable to cry or to move, only a creeping numbness as I heard myself say, what now seemed like a hundred years ago, "Are you going back to medicine?" His words came flooding back.

"No, there's something important I have to do first."

And then I knew.

He'd really no choice, he had to go. This thing was interfering with his life, the difference between what you feel you want to do. And what you feel you must do and he had to do it on his terms. Oh, God! How I hated that brash American! How could a person with absolutely no principles about some things, have such high and mighty ones about others? In unbearable pain and frustration, I banged my fists down on the boiler, with that same ferocity as I did that night on his bedroom wall and the result was the same... Silence!

It was Shelagh who spoke eventually, most of the others leaving quietly.

"I'm so sorry Pao, I know how very special he was to you." Her words were an unwelcome invasion in my nightmare. "Don't call me that! Don't anyone ever call me that again!" I screamed. She gently replaced the letter in my hand, closing my fingers around it. "We'll leave you alone now, okay?"

"Thanks," I whispered.

And everyone left me alone in the kitchen with my pain and overwhelming sense of loss, Shelagh the last to leave, closing the door quietly behind her.

***

I read the letter over and over again, trying to find some little word, some small reason, which would make the pain go away. His Mother said, they had only a short time together after he'd arrived home, but during that time he had talked a great deal about England. He told her that everything had become clear but he would never be truly at peace unless he went to the war to see for himself. He said that he had to see the people, their faces, their children and the way they lived and if they really were a threat to the great 'Uncle Sam'. He was convinced that if he could only see the people, then somehow it would all be all right.

I wondered if he had ever done that.

The cat crept up and settled on my lap and I stroked her soft fur remembering the first moment I saw him, his voice bouncing around, mercilessly in my head.

"Trust me, Ma-am, I know a little bit about these things!" And then I wept until there were no tears left to cry. I cried for Robbie and for me, for all the old men and the little children and for all the beautiful sunsets that he would never see.

What a waste! What a bloody awful waste! Then came the anger and I cried aloud. "Damn you, Robbie, damn you to hell! Damn your conscience and your lousy reconciliations. Why did you have to go and why did you have to leave me?" My head bent forward, arms cuddling the cat.

"Help me someone please, anyone, anyone please."

"Hey, Ma-am, you only gotta ask."

That voice inside my head again! Or was it? The cat, startled, sank her claws into the soft skin of my leg and jumped onto the window ledge, giving a brief hiss, her ears flattened.

Slowly, deliberately, I got down from the boiler, listening intently as there came from behind me, the faintest waft of perfume, Blue Grass! As I looked over my shoulder, a warm sensation, like the embrace of strong arms enveloped me and I remembered just when I had felt like that before.

Linnie had brought him back to me, just for a few seconds, but I had no doubt that he was there in the kitchen, come to hold me one last time.

I made cocoa, or was it chocolate perhaps? And standing there in the darkness, I knew that Robbie was okay and that he had done all that he had set out to do, so by what right did I shed tears for him?

"Be happy whenever you think of me," he had said. I read the letter once more, his words echoing in my head. "Tell them we are just ordinary people Pao. We work, play, love and chase women just like everybody else. Tell them we're not different, just ordinary folk with a bit of extra insight and talent that's all. Do it for me… tell the story!"

I turned and looked out of the window at the frosty night full of stars, wondering which one was his and as I looked, a profound sense of peace settled all around me and I promised.

"Yes, Robbie, I will do it, one day! For you, for me, and for friendship," and smiling at last, folded the letter carefully and put it in my pocket.

Also by Sue Pacey

http://getbook.at/cradle

About Sue Pacey

I have been writing a long time, usually for pleasure. Twelve years ago, with the end of a very long career in midwifery approaching – though it hasn't yet – I joined a local writer's group, led by Paul Kane, a successful writer himself. Of the thirteen members, ten of us rapidly became published authors.

Our first anthology won the prestigious David St John Thomas Award run by the Society of Authors in 2007. Some of us novelists are still together, meeting fortnightly to review each other's work.

My first novel, the first of a trilogy, *Listening to Linnie*, was first published in 2014. The sequel is completed, and the third, well on the way. In February 2017, my second novel, *A Silent Cradle*, was published.

From my almost 50-year career, I have so much material that demands to be written down and shared. The genre? Well, it's a bit like *Call the Midwife* meets *The Sixth Sense*. I've always had an abiding interest in both the paranormal and nursing. It seemed natural to combine the two. Judging by the comments on Amazon, it's a winning mix.

Printed in Great Britain
by Amazon